The Man from Home

**Booth Tarkington
& Harry Leon Wilson**

The Man from Home

Copyright © 2020 Bibliotech Press
All rights reserved

The present edition is a reproduction of previous publication of this classic work. Minor typographical errors may have been corrected without note; however, for an authentic reading experience the spelling, punctuation, and capitalization have been retained from the original text.

ISBN: 978-1-64799-894-3

TO

WILLIAM HODGE

CONTENTS

ORIGINAL CAST OF CHARACTERS

IN

THE MAN FROM HOME

BY
BOOTH TARKINGTON and HARRY LEON WILSON

PRESENTED UNDER THE MANAGEMENT OF LIEBLER & CO.

AT THE

STUDEBAKER THEATRE, CHICAGO

SEPTEMBER 29, 1907

WHERE IT RAN FOR A YEAR; THEN OPENED IN NEW YORK
AT THE
ASTOR THEATRE

AUGUST 17, 1908

CHARACTERS AND PLAYERS

Daniel Voorhees Pike	William Hodge
The Grand Duke Vasili Vasilivitch	Eben Plympton
The Earl of Hawcastle	E. J. Ratcliffe
The Hon. Alermic St. Aubyn	Echlin P. Gayer
Ivanoff	Henry Harmon
Horace Granger-Simpson	Hassard Short
Ribiere	Harry L. Lang
Mariano	Anthony Asher
Michele	Antonio Salerno
Carabiniere	A. Montegriffo

1

Valet de Chambre	C. L. Felton
Ethel Granger-Simpson	Olive Wyndam
Comtesse de Champigny	Alice Johnson
Lady Creech	Ida Vernon

TIME: THE PRESENT

PLACE: SORRENTO, SOUTHERN ITALY

2

CHARACTERS

MEN

DANIEL VOORHEES PIKE
Of Kokomo, Indiana

THE GRAND-DUKE VASILI VASILIVITCH

THE EARL OF HAWCASTLE

THE HON. ALMERIC ST. AUBYN
Son of Lord Hawcastle

IVANOFF

HORACE GRANGER-SIMPSON

RIBIERE
The Grand-Duke's secretary

MARIANO
Maître d'hôtel

MICHELE
A waiter

Two carabiniere

A valet de chambre

Several Sorrentine musicians and fishermen

WOMEN

ETHEL GRANGER-SIMPSON

COMTESSE DE CHAMPIGNY

LADY CREECH
Sister-in-law of Hawcastle

The time is the present.

The scene is Sorrento, in Southern Italy.

3

THE FIRST ACT

SCENE: The terrace of the Hotel Regina Margherita, on the cliff at Sorrento, overlooking the Bay of Naples.

There is a view of the bay and its semi-circular coast-line, dotted with villages; Vesuvius gray in the distance. Across the stage at the rear runs a marble balustrade about three feet high, guarding the edge of the cliff. Upon the left is seen part of one wing of the hotel, entrance to which is afforded by wide-open double doors approached by four or five marble steps with a railing and small stoop. The hotel is of pink and white stucco, and striped awnings shield the windows. Upon the right is a lemon grove and shrubberies. There are two or three small white wicker tea-tables and a number of wicker chairs upon the left, and a square table laid with white cloth on the right.

As the curtain rises mandolins and guitars are heard, and the "Fisherman's Song," the time very rapid and gay, the musicians being unseen.

MARIANO, maître d'hôtel, is discovered laying the table down R.C. with eggs, coffee, and rolls for two. He is a pleasant-faced, elderly man, stout, swarthy, clean shaven; wears dress-clothes, white waist-coat, and black tie. He is annoyed by the music.

MARIANO

[calling to the unseen musicians crossly]

Silenzio!

[MICHELE enters from the hotel. He is young, clean-shaven except for a dark mustache, wears a white tie, a blue coat, cut like dress-coat, blue trousers with red side stripes, brass buttons; his waistcoat is of striped red and blue.]

MICHELE

[speaking over his shoulder]

Par ici, Monsieur Ribiere, pour le maître d'hôtel.

4

[RIBIERE enters from the hotel.]

[MICHELE immediately withdraws.]

[RIBIERE is a trim, business-like young Frenchman of some distinction of appearance. He wears a well-made English dark "cutaway" walking-suit, a derby hat, and carries a handsome leather writing-case under his arm.]

RIBIERE

[as he enters]

Ah, Mariano!

MARIANO

[bowing and greeting him gayly]

Monsieur Ribiere! J'espère que vous êtes—

[He breaks off, turns on his heel toward the invisible musicians, and shouts.]

Silenzio!

[He turns again quickly to RIBIERE.]

RIBIERE

[with a warning glance toward hotel]

Let us speak English. There are not so many who understand.

MARIANO

[politely]

I hope Monsieur still occupy the exalt' position of secretar' to Monseigneur the Grand-Duke.

RIBIERE

[sits and opens writing-case, answers gravely]

We will not mention the name or rank of my employer.

5

MARIANO

[with gesture and accent of despair]

Again incognito! Every year he come to our hotel for two, three day, but always incognito.

[He finishes setting the table.]

We lose the honor to have it known.

RIBIERE

[looking at his watch]

He comes in his automobile from Naples. Everything is to be as on my employer's former visits—strictly incognito. It is understood every one shall address him as Herr von Gröllerhagen—

MARIANO

[repeating the name carefully]

Herr von Gröllerhagen—

RIBIERE

He wishes to be thought a German.

[Takes a note-book from case.]

MARIANO

Such a man! of caprice? Excentrique? Ha!

RIBIERE

You have said it. Last night he talked by chance to a singular North American in the hotel at Napoli. To-day he has that stranger for companion in the automobile. I remonstrate. What use? He laugh for half an hour!

MARIANO

He is not like those cousin of his at St. Petersburg an' Moscowa. An' yet though Monseigneur is so good an' generoso, will not the anarchist strike against the name of royalty himself? You have not the fear?

6

RIBIERE

[opening his note-book]

I have. He has *not*. I take what precaution I can secretly from him. You have few guests?

MARIANO

[smiling]

It is so early in the season. Those poor musician'

[nodding off right]

they wait always at every gate, to play when they see any one coming. There is only seex peoples in the 'ole house! All of one party.

RIBIERE

Good! Who are they?

MARIANO

There is Milor', an English Excellency—the Earl of Hawcastle; there is his son, the Excellency Honorabile Almeric St. Aubyn; there is Miladi Creeshe, an English Miladi who is sister-in-law to Milor' Hawcastle.

RIBIERE

[taking notes]

Three English.

MARIANO

There is an American Signorina, Mees Granger-Seempsone. Miladi Creeshe travel with her to be chaperone.

[Enthusiastically.]

She is young, generosa, she give money to every one, she is multa bella, so pretty, weeth charm—

RIBIERE

[puzzled]

You speak now of Lady Creeshe?

MARIANO

[taken aback]

Oh no, no, no! Miladi Creeshe is ol' lady

[tapping his ears]

Not hear well. Deaf. No pourboires. Nothing. I speak of the young American lady, Mees Granger-Seempsone who the English Honorabile son of Milor' Hawcastle wish to espouse, I think.

RIBIERE

Who else is there?

MARIANO

There is the brother of Mees Granger-Seempsone, a young gentleman of North America. He make the eyes

[laughing]

all day at another lady who is of the party, a French lady, Comtesse de Champigny. Ha, ha! That amuse' me!

RIBIERE

Why?

MARIANO

Beckoss I think Comtesse de Champigny is a such good friend of the ol' English Milor' Hawcastle. A maître d'hôtel see many things, an' I think Milor' Hawcastle and Madame de Champigny have know each other from long, perhaps. This déjeuner is for them.

RIBIERE

And who else?

8

MARIANO

It is all.

RIBIERE

Good! no Russians?

MARIANO

I think Milor' Hawcastle and Madame de Champigny have been in Russia sometime.

RIBIERE

[putting his note-book in his pocket]

Why?

MARIANO

Beckoss once I have hear them spik Russian togezzer.

RIBIERE

I think there is small chance that they recognize my employer. His portrait is little known.

MARIANO

And this North American who come in the automobile—does *he* know who he travel wiz? Does he know his Highness?

RIBIERE

No more than the baby which is not borned.

MARIANO

[lifting his eyes to heaven]

Ah!

RIBIERE

[looking at his watch]

Set déjeuner on the terrace instantly when he arrive: a perch, petit

9

pois, iced figs, tea. I will send his own caviar and vodka from the supplies I carry.

MARIANO

I set for one?

RIBIERE

For two. He desires that the North American breakfast with him. Do not forget that the incognito is to be absolute.

[Exit into hotel.]

MARIANO

Va bene, Signore!

[Puts finishing-touches to the table.]

[Enter from the grove, LORD HAWCASTLE. He is a well-preserved man of fifty-six with close-clipped gray mustache and gray hair; his eyes are quick and shrewd; his face shows some slight traces of high living; he carries himself well and his general air is distinguished and high-bred. He wears a suit of thinly striped white flannel and white shoes, a four-in-hand tie of pale old-rose crape, a Panama hat with broad ribbon striped with white and old-rose of the same shade as his tie. His accent is that of a man of the world, and quite without affectation. He comes at once upon his entrance to a chair at the table.]

[MICHELE enters at same time up left, with a folded newspaper.]

HAWCASTLE

[as he enters]

Good-morning, Mariano!

MARIANO

[bowing]

Milor' Hawcastle is serve.

[Takes HAWCASTLE'S hat and places it upon a stool behind table.]

MICHELE

[hands HAWCASTLE newspaper from under his arm]

Il Mattino, the morning journal from Napoli, Milor'.

HAWCASTLE

[accepting paper and unfolding it]

No English papers?

MICHELE

Milor', the mail is late.

[Exit up left.]

HAWCASTLE

[sitting]

And Madame de Champigny?

[MARIANO serves coffee, etc.]

[As HAWCASTLE speaks the COMTESSE DE CHAMPIGNY enters from hotel. She is a pretty Frenchwoman of thirty-two. She wears a fashionable summer Parisian morning dress, light and gay in color, a short-sleeved little Empire jacket, and long gloves. She carries a parasol. Her elaborately dressed hair is surmounted by a jaunty Parisian toque.]

MADAME DE CHAMPIGNY

[lifting her hand gayly as she enters, and striking a little attitude before she descends the steps]

Me voici!

HAWCASTLE

[half rising and bowing]

My esteemed relative is still asleep?

MADAME DE CHAMPIGNY

[speaking gayly, with a very slight accent, as she crosses to a chair at the table]

I trust your beautiful son has found much better employment—as our hearts would wish him to.

HAWCASTLE

He has. He's off on a canter with the little American, thank God!

MADAME DE CHAMPIGNY

[interjecting the word]

Bravo!

[She turns the hands of her gloves back and sips coffee, MARIANO serving.]

HAWCASTLE

[continuing]

But I didn't mean Almeric. I meant my august sister-in-law.

[He reads the paper.]

MADAME DE CHAMPIGNY

[smiling]

The amiable Lady Victoria Hermione Trevelyan Creech has déjeuner in her apartment. What you find to read?

HAWCASTLE

I'm such a duffer at Italian, but apparently the people along the coast are having a scare over an escaped convict—a Russian.

MARIANO

[starting slightly, drops a spoon noisily upon a plate on the table]

Pardon, Milor'!

MADAME DE CHAMPIGNY

[setting down her coffee abruptly]

A Russian?

HAWCASTLE

[translating with difficulty]

"An escaped Russian bandit has been traced to Castellamare—"

[Pauses.]

MARIANO

[awe-struck]

Castellamare—not twelve kilometres from here!

HAWCASTLE

[continuing]

"—and a confidential agent"—

[looking up]

—secret-service man, I dare say—"has requested his arrest. But the brigand tore himself"—

[repeating slowly]

—"tore himself"—What the deuce does that mean?

MARIANO

[bowing]

Pardon, Milor'—if I might—

HAWCASTLE

Quite right, Mariano!

[Handing him the paper.]

Translate for us.

13

MARIANO

[reading rapidly, but with growing agitation which he tries to conceal]

"The brigan' tore himself from the hands of the carabiniere and without the doubts he conceal himself in some of those grotto near Sorrento and searchment is being execute'. The agent of the Russian embassy have inform' the bureau that this escaped one is a mos' in-fay-mose robber and danger brigand."

MADAME DE CHAMPIGNY

[quickly]

What name does the journal say he has?

MARIANO

[hurriedly]

It has not to say. That is all. Will Milor' and Madame la Comtesse excuse me? And may I take the journal? There is one who should see it.

HAWCASTLE

[indifferently]

Very well.

MARIANO

Thank you, Milor'!

[Bows hastily and hurries out up left.]

MADAME DE CHAMPIGNY

[gravely, drawing back from the table.]

I should like much to know his name.

HAWCASTLE

[smiling, and eating composedly]

14

You may be sure it isn't Ivanoff.

MADAME DE CHAMPIGNY

[not changing her attitude]

How can one know it is not

[pauses and speaks the name very gravely]

Ivanoff?

HAWCASTLE

[laughing]

He wouldn't be called an infamous brigand.

MADAME DE CHAMPIGNY

[very gravely]

That, my friend, may be only Italian journalism.

HAWCASTLE

Pooh! This means a highwayman—

[finishes his coffee coolly]

—not—not an embezzler, Hélène.

MADAME DE CHAMPIGNY

[taking a deep breath and sinking back in her chair with a fixed gaze]

I am glad to believe it, but I care for no more to eat. I have some foolish feeling of unsafety. It is now two nights that I dream of him—of Ivanoff—bad dreams for us both, my friend.

HAWCASTLE

[laughing]

What rot! It takes more than a dream to bring a man back from Siberia.

MADAME DE CHAMPIGNY

Then I pray there has been no more than dreams.

[Music of mandolins and guitars heard off to the right with song— "The Fisherman's Song."]

[Enter ETHEL gayly and quickly from the grove, her face radiant. She is a very pretty American girl of twenty. She wears a light-brown linen skirted coat, fitting closely, and a country riding-skirt of the same material and color, with boots, a shirt-waist, collar and tie, and three-cornered hat. She carries a riding-crop. She is followed by three musicians (two mandolins and a guitar), who laughingly continue the song. They are shabby fellows, two of them barefooted, wearing shabby, patched velveteen trousers and blue flannel shirts open at the throat, with big black hats, old and shapeless. One makes a low and sweeping bow before ETHEL; she takes money from her glove and gives it to him, the other two not discontinuing the song; the three immediately 'bout face and go out gleefully, capering and still singing.]

HAWCASTLE

[who has risen]

The divine Miss Granger-Simpson!

ETHEL

[with a pronounced "English accent"]

The divinely happy Miss Granger-Simpson!

MADAME DE CHAMPIGNY

[rising, running to her, and kissing her]

Oh, I hope you mean—

HAWCASTLE

[with some excitement in his voice]

You mean you have made my son divinely happy?

[ETHEL, as he speaks, extricates herself laughingly from MADAME DE CHAMPIGNY.]

16

ETHEL

Is not every one happy in Sorrento—

[with a wave of her riding-crop]

—even your son?

[Exit laughingly and hurriedly into the hotel.]

[MADAME DE CHAMPIGNY goes to stool behind table and gets her parasol, as HAWCASTLE resumes his seat.]

MADAME DE CHAMPIGNY

Ah! that is good. Listen!

[A piano sounds from the room ETHEL has just entered, breaking loudly and gayly into Chaminade's "Elevation." ETHEL'S voice is heard for a moment, also, singing.]

She has flown to her piano. It looks well, indeed—our little enterprise.

HAWCASTLE

[grimly]

It's time. If Almeric had been anything but a clumsy oof he'd have made her settle it weeks ago!

MADAME DE CHAMPIGNY

[quickly]

You are invidious, mon ami! My affair is not settled—am *I* a clumsy oof?

HAWCASTLE

[leaning toward her across the table and speaking sharply and earnestly]

No, Hélène. *Your* little American, brother Horace, is so in love with you, if you asked him suddenly, "Is this day or night?" he would answer, "It's Hélène." But he's too shy to speak. You're a woman—you can't press matters; but Almeric's a man—he can. He can urge

17

an immediate marriage, which means an immediate settlement, and a direct one.

MADAME DE CHAMPIGNY

[seriously, quickly]

It will not be small, that settlement?

[He shakes his head grimly, leaning back to look at her. She continues eagerly.]

You have decide' what sum?

[He nods decidedly.]

What?

HAWCASTLE

[sharply, with determination, yet quietly]

A hundred and fifty thousand pounds!

MADAME DE CHAMPIGNY

[excited and breathless]

My friend! Will she?

[Turns and stares toward ETHEL'S room, where the piano is still heard softly playing.]

HAWCASTLE

Not for Almeric, but to be the future Countess of Hawcastle. My sister-in-law hasn't been her chaperone for a year for nothing. And, by Jove, she hasn't done it for nothing, either!

[He laughs grimly, moving back from the table.]

But she's deserved all I shall allow her.

MADAME DE CHAMPIGNY

[coldly]

Why?

HAWCASTLE

[rising]

It was she who found these people. Indeed, we might say that both you and I owe her something also.

[Comes around behind table to MADAME DE CHAMPIGNY.]

Even a less captious respectability than Lady Creech's might have looked askance at the long friendship

[kisses her hand]

which has existed between us. Yet she has always countenanced us, though she must have guessed—a great many things. And she will help us to urge an immediate marriage. You know as well as I do that unless it is immediate, there'll be the devil to pay. Don't miss *that* essential: something must be done at once. We're at the breaking-point—if you like the words—a most damnable insolvency.

[Enter ALMERIC from the grove. He is a fair, fresh-colored Englishman of twenty-five, handsome in a rather vacuous way. He wears white duck riding-breeches, light-tan leather riding-gaiters and shoes, a riding-coat of white duck, a waistcoat light tan in shade, and a high riding-stock, the collar of which is white, the "puffed" tie pink; a Panama hat with a fold of light tan and white silk round the crown. Carries a riding-crop.]

ALMERIC

[as he enters]

Hello, Governor!

[His voice is habitually loud and his accent somewhat foppish, having a little of the "Guardsman" affectation of languor and indifference.]

Howdy, Countess!

[He drops into a chair at the breakfast-table with a slight effect of sprawling.]

HAWCASTLE

[sharply]

19

Almeric!

ALMERIC

Out riding a bit ago, you know, with Miss Granger-Simpson. Rippin' girl, *isn't* she?

HAWCASTLE

[leaning across the table toward him, anxiously]

Go on!

ALMERIC

[continuing, slapping his gaiters carelessly with his crop]

Didn't stop with her, though.

HAWCASTLE

[angrily]

Why not?

ALMERIC

A sort of man in the village got me to go look at a bull-terrier pup. Wonderful little beast for points. Jolly luck—*wasn't* it? He's got a *head* on him—

HAWCASTLE

[bitterly]

We'll concede his *tremendous* advantage over you in that respect.

[Throws his cigar disgustedly into one of the coffee-cups on the table.]

MADAME DE CHAMPIGNY

[eagerly]

Is that *all* you have to tell us?

20

ALMERIC

Oh no! She accepted me.

[HAWCASTLE drops into a chair with a long breath of relief.]

MADAME DE CHAMPIGNY

[waving her parasol]

Enfin! Bravo! And will she let it be soon?

ALMERIC

[sincerely]

I dare say there'll be no row about that; I've made her aw'fly happy.

HAWCASTLE

On my soul, I believe you're right—and thank God you are!

[Rises as he speaks and walks up centre. Breaks off short as he sees HORACE.]

Here's the brother—attention now!

[HORACE enters the hotel. He is a boyish-looking American of twenty-two, smooth-shaven. He wears white flannels, the coat double-breasted and buttoned, the tie is light blue "puffing" fastened with a large pearl. He wears light-yellow chamois gloves, white shoes, a small, stiff English straw hat with blue-and-white ribbon. When he speaks it is with a strong "English accent," which he sometimes forgets. At present he is flushed and almost overcome with happy emotion. As he comes down the steps MADAME DE CHAMPIGNY rushes toward him, taking both his hands.]

MADAME DE CHAMPIGNY

[excitedly]

Ah, my dear Horace Granger-Simpson! Has your sister told you?

HORACE

[radiant, but almost tearful]

She has, indeed. I assure you I'm quite overcome.

21

[MADAME DE CHAMPIGNY, dropping his hands, laughs deprecatingly, and steps back from him.]

Really, I assure you.

HAWCASTLE

[shaking hands with him very heartily]

My dear young friend, not at all, not at all.

HORACE

[fanning himself with his hat and wiping his brow]

I assure you I am, I assure you I am—it's quite overpowering—*isn't it?*

MADAME DE CHAMPIGNY

Ah, poor Monsieur Horace!

ALMERIC

I say, don't take it that way, you know. She's very happy.

HORACE

[crossing and grasping his hand]

She's worthy of it—she's worthy of it. I know she is. And when will it be?

MADAME DE CHAMPIGNY

Enchanting.

HAWCASTLE

Oh, the date? I dare say within a year—two years—

[COMTESSE starts to exclaim, but HAWCASTLE checks her.]

HORACE

Oh, but I say, you know! Isn't that putting it jolly far off? The thing's settled, isn't it? Why not say a month instead of a year?

HAWCASTLE

Oh, if you like, I don't know that there is any real objection.

HORACE

I do like, indeed. Why not let them marry here in Italy?

HAWCASTLE

Ah, the dashing methods of you Americans! Next you'll be saying, "Why not here at Sorrento?"

HORACE

Well, and why not, indeed?

HAWCASTLE

And then it will be, "Why not within a fortnight?"

HORACE

And why should it not be in a fortnight?

HAWCASTLE

Ah, you wonderful people, you are whirlwinds, yet I see no reason why it should not be in a fortnight.

ALMERIC

[passively]

Just as you like, Governor, just as you like.

MADAME DE CHAMPIGNY

Enchanting.

HAWCASTLE

My son is all impatience!

ALMERIC

[genially]

Quite so!

HAWCASTLE

[gayly]

Shall we dispose at once of the necessary little details, the various minor arrangements, the—the settlement?

[Interrupts himself with a friendly laugh.]

Of course, as a man of the world, of *our* world, you understand there *are* formalities in the nature of a settlement.

HORACE

[interrupting eagerly and pleasantly, laughing also]

Quite so, of course, I know, certainly, perfectly!

HAWCASTLE

[heartily]

We'll have no difficulty about *that*, my boy. I'll wire my solicitor immediately, and he'll be here within two days. If you wish to consult your own solicitor you can cable him.

HORACE

[with some embarrassment]

Fact is, I've a notion our solicitor—Ethel's man of business, that is— from Kokomo, Indiana, where our Governor lived—in fact, a sort of guardian of hers—may be here almost any time.

HAWCASTLE

[taken aback]

A sort of guardian—*what* sort?

HORACE

[apologetically]

I really can't say. Never saw him that I know of. You see, we've been on this side so many years, and there's been no occasion for this fellow to look us up, but he's never opposed anything Ethel wrote for; he seems to be an easygoing old chap.

24

HAWCASTLE

[anxiously]

But would his consent to your sister's marriage—or the matter of a settlement—be a necessity?

HORACE

[easily]

Oh, I dare say; but if he has the slightest sense of duty toward my sister, he'll be the first to welcome the alliance, won't he?

HAWCASTLE

[reassured]

Then when my solicitor comes, he and your man can have an evening over a lot of musty papers and the thing will be done. Again, my boy,

[taking HORACE'S hand]

I welcome you to our family. God bless you!

HORACE

I'm overpowered, you know—really overpowered.

[Fans himself again and wipes his forehead.]

HAWCASTLE

Come, Almeric.

[Aside to MADAME DE CHAMPIGNY, whom he joins for a moment.]

Let him know it's a hundred and fifty thousand pounds.

[Exit into hotel, followed immediately by ALMERIC.]

[HORACE turns toward MADAME DE CHAMPIGNY; she gives him both hands.]

MADAME DE CHAMPIGNY

[smiling]

My friend, I am happy for you.

HORACE

[joyously]

Think of it, at the most a fortnight, and dear old Ethel will be the Honorable Mrs. St. Aubyn, future Countess of Hawcastle!

[MADAME DE CHAMPIGNY, lightly, at the same time withdrawing her hands and picking up her parasol from the chair where she has left it.]

MADAME DE CHAMPIGNY

Yes, there is but those little arrangement over the settlement paper between your advocate and Lord Hawcastle's; but you Americans— you laugh at such things. You are big, so big, like your country!

HORACE

Ah, believe me, the great world, the world of yourself, Countess, has thoroughly alienated me.

MADAME DE CHAMPIGNY

[coming close to him, looking at him admiringly]

Ah, you retain one quality! You are big, you are careless, you are free.

[She lays her right hand on his left arm. He takes her hand with his right hand. They stand facing each other.]

HORACE

[smiling]

Well, perhaps, in *those* things I am American, but in others I fancy I should be thought something else, shouldn't I?

MADAME DE CHAMPIGNY

[earnestly]

You are a debonair man of the great world; and yet you are still American, in that you are ab-om-i-nab-ly rich.

[She laughs sweetly.]

The settlement—Such matter as that, over which a Frenchman, an Italian, an Englishman might hesitate, you laugh! Such matter as one-hundred-fifty thousand pounds—you set it aside; you laugh! You say, "Oh yes—take it!"

HORACE

[his eyes wide with surprise]

A hundred and fifty thousand pounds! Why, that's seven hundred and fifty thous—

[He pauses, then finishes decidedly.]

She couldn't use the money to better advantage.

[Enter ETHEL from the hotel. She has one thick book under her arm, another in her hand.]

MADAME DE CHAMPIGNY

[to HORACE, with deep admiration]

My friend, how wise you are!

[She perceives ETHEL'S entrance over HORACE'S shoulder, and at once runs to her, embraces her, and kisses her, crying.]

Largesse, sweet Countess of Hawcastle! Largesse! and au revoir! Adieu! I leave you with your dear brother. A riverderci.

[She runs gayly out, waving her parasol to them as she goes.]

HORACE

[going to ETHEL]

Dear old sis, dear old pal!

[Affectionately gives her hand a squeeze and drops it.]

ETHEL

[radiant]

Isn't it glorious, Hoddy!

HORACE

The others are almost as pleased as we are.

[He leans back in chair, knees crossed, hands clasped over knees, and regards her proudly.]

ETHEL

[opens the books she carries, laying them on one of the tea-tables]

This is Burke's *Peerage*, and this is Froissart's *Chronicles*. I've been reading it all over again—the St. Aubyns at Crecy and Agincourt,

[with an exalted expression]

and St. Aubyn will be *my* name!

HORACE

[smiling]

They want it to be your name *soon*, sis.

ETHEL

[suddenly thoughtful, speaks appealingly]

You're fond of Almeric, aren't you, Hoddy—*you* admire him, don't you?

HORACE

Certainly. Think of all he represents.

ETHEL

[enthusiastically]

Ah, yes! Crusader's blood flows in his veins. It is to the nobility that *must* be within him that I have plighted my troth. I am ready to marry him when they wish.

HORACE

Then as soon as the settlement is arranged. It'll take about all your share of the estate, sis, but it's worth it—a hundred and fifty thousand pounds.

ETHEL

[earnestly]

What better use could be made of a fortune than to maintain the state and high condition of so ancient a house?

HORACE

Doesn't it seem impossible that we were born in Indiana!

[He speaks seriously, as if the thing were incredible.]

ETHEL

[smiling]

But isn't it good that the pater "made his pile," as the Americans say, and let us come over here when we were young to find the nobler things, Hoddy—the *nobler* things!

HORACE

The nobler things—the nobler things, sis. When old Hawcastle dies I'll be saying, quite off-hand, you know, "My sister, the Countess of Hawcastle—"

ETHEL

[thoughtfully]

You don't suppose that father's friend, my guardian, this old Mr. Pike, will be—will be QUEER, do you?

HORACE

Well, the governor himself was rather *raw*, you know. This is probably a harmless enough old chap—easy to handle—

29

ETHEL

I wish I knew. I shouldn't like Almeric's family to think we had queer connections of any sort—and he might turn out to be quite shockingly American

[with genuine pathos]

I—I couldn't bear it, Hoddy.

HORACE

Then keep him out of the way. That's simple enough. None of them, except the solicitor, need see him.

[Instantly upon this there is a tremendous though distant commotion beyond the hotel—wild laughter and cheers, the tarantella played by mandolins and guitars, also sung, shouts of "Bravo Americano!" and "Yanka Dooda!" The noise continues and increases gradually.]

ETHEL

[as the uproar begins]

What is that?

HORACE

Must be a mob.

[LADY CREECH, flustered and hot, enters from the hotel. She is a haughty, cross-looking woman in the sixties.]

ETHEL

[going to LADY CREECH, speaks close to her ear and loudly]

Lady Creech—dear Lady Creech—what is the trouble?

LADY CREECH

Some horrible people coming to this hotel! They've made a riot in the village.

[The noise becomes suddenly louder. MARIANO, immediately upon

LADY CREECH'S entrance, appears in hotel doors, makes a quick gesture toward breakfast-table, and withdraws.]

[MICHELE, laughing, immediately enters by same doors, goes rapidly to the breakfast-table and clears it. The others pay no attention to this.]

HORACE

[at steps up left]

It's not a riot—it's a revolution.

LADY CREECH

[sinking into a chair, angrily]

One of your horrid fellow-countrymen, my dear. Your Americans are really too—

ETHEL

[proudly]

Not *my* Americans, Lady Creech!

HORACE

Not *ours*, you know. One could hardly say that, *could* one?

ALMERIC

[heard outside laughing]

Oh, I say, what a go!

[Enters from the hotel, laughing.]

Motor-car breaks down on the way here; one of the Johnnies in it, a German, discharges the chauffeur; and the other Johnny,

[he throws himself sprawling into a chair]

one of your Yankee chaps, Ethel, hires two silly little donkeys, like rabbits, you know, to pull the machine the rest of the way here. Then as they can't make it, by Jove, you know, he puts himself in the straps with the donkeys, and proceeds, attended by the populace. Ha, ha! I say!

[HORACE, gloomy, comes down and sits at tea-table.]

LADY CREECH

[angrily, to ALMERIC]

Don't mumble your words, Almeric. I never understand people when they mumble their words.

[RIBIERE, who looks anxious, appears in the hotel doorway, then stands aside on the stoop for MARIANO and MICHELE; they enter and pass him with trays, fresh cloth, etc., for table down right, which they rapidly proceed to set. A valet de chambre enters up left, following them immediately. He carries a tray with a silver dish of caviar and a bottle of vodka. As he enters he hesitates for one moment, looking inquiringly at RIBIERE, who motions him quickly toward MARIANO and MICHELE, and withdraws. Valet rapidly crosses right to table, sets caviar and vodka on the table, and exits up left. The others pay no attention to any of this.]

ALMERIC

I went up to this Yankee chap, I mean to say—he was pullin' and tuggin' along, you see, don't you?—and I said, "There you are, three of you all in a row, *aren't* you?"—meanin' him and the two donkeys, Ethel, you see.

LADY CREECH

[who has been leaning close to ALMERIC to listen]

Dreadful person!

ALMERIC

[continuing]

All he could answer was that he'd picked the best company in sight.

ETHEL

[annoyed, half under her breath]

Impertinent!

32

ALMERIC

No meanin' to it. I had him, you know, I rather think, didn't I?

[HAWCASTLE enters with MADAME DE CHAMPIGNY, a number of folded newspapers under his arm. Simultaneously loud cheers are heard from the village and a general renewal of the commotion.]

HAWCASTLE

Disgusting uproar!

MADAME DE CHAMPIGNY

[to ETHEL]

But we know that such Americans are not of your class, cherie.

ETHEL

A dreadful person, I quite fear.

HAWCASTLE

The English papers.

[Lays papers on one of the tea-tables.]

ALMERIC

I'll take the *Pink 'Un*, Governor. I'm off.

[Starts to go, the *Pink 'Un* under his arm.]

ETHEL

[rather shyly]

For a stroll, Almeric? Would you like me to go with you?

ALMERIC

[somewhat embarrassed]

Well, I rather thought I'd have a quiet bit of readin', you know.

33

ETHEL

[coldly]

Oh!

[Exit ALMERIC rapidly up left.]

LADY CREECH

[in a deep and gloomy voice]

The *Church Register*!

[HAWCASTLE gives her a paper.]

[HORACE takes the London *Mail*.]

[HAWCASTLE takes the *Times*.]

[ETHEL and MADAME DE CHAMPIGNY walk back to the terrace railing, chatting. The others seat themselves about the tea-tables to read.]

HORACE

[unfolding his paper, speaks crossly to MARIANO]

Mariano, how long is this noise to continue?

MARIANO

[distractedly]

How can I know? We can do nothing.

MICHELE

[smilingly, looking up from table where he has continued to work]

The people outside will not go while they think there is once more a chance to see the North American who pull the automobile with those donkeys.

MARIANO

He have confuse' me; he have confuse' everybody. He will not be content with the déjeuner till he have the ham and the eggs. And he will have the eggs cooked only on one side, and how in the name of heaven can we tell which side?

RIBIERE

[appearing in the hotel doorway, speaks sharply but not loudly]

Garçon!

[MICHELE and MARIANO instantly step back from table and stand at attention, facing front, like soldiers. RIBIERE exits quickly again into hotel.]

HAWCASTLE

[looking up from paper]

Upon my soul, who's all this?

MARIANO

[not turning his head, replies in an awed undertone]

It is Herr von Gröllerhagen, a German gentleman, Milor'.

HAWCASTLE

[amused, to HORACE]

Man that owned the automobile. Probably made a fortune in sausages.

VASILI

[heard within the hotel, approaching]

Nein, nein, Ribiere! 'S macht nichts!

[He enters from the hotel. He is a portly man of forty-five, but rather soldierly than fat. His hair, pompadour, is reddish blond, beginning to turn gray, like his mustache and large full beard; the latter somewhat "Henry IV." and slightly forked at bottom. His dress produces the effect rather of carelessness than of extreme fashion. He wears a travelling-suit of gray, neat enough but not freshly pressed, the trousers showing no crease, the coat cut in "walking-coat style," with big, slanting pockets, in which he carries his gloves, handkerchief, matches, and a silver cigarette-case full of

35

Russian cigarettes. On his head is a tan-colored automobile cap with buttoned flaps. He is followed by RIBIERE, who, anxious and perturbed, wishes to call his attention to the item in the Neapolitan morning paper.]

VASILI

[waving both RIBIERE and the paper aside, in high good-humor]

Las' mich, las' mich! Geh'n sie weg!

[RIBIERE bows submissively, though with a gesture of protest, and exit into the hotel. The group about the tea-table watch VASILI with hostility.]

LADY CREECH

What a dreadful person!

[VASILI crosses to his seat at the breakfast-table in front of MARIANO and MICHELE, who bows profoundly as he passes.]

VASILI

[lifting his hand in curt, semi-military salute, to acknowledge the waiters' bows]

See to my American friend.

[MICHELE immediately hastens into the hotel. VASILI sits, and MARIANO serves him.]

HAWCASTLE

[to LADY CREECH, in her ear]

Quite right; but take care, he speaks English.

LADY CREECH

[glaring at VASILI]

Many thoroughly objectionable persons do!

VASILI

[apparently oblivious to her remark, to MARIANO]

My American friend wishes his own national dish.

MARIANO

[deferentially, and serving VASILI to caviar]

Yes, Herr von Gröllerhagen, he will have the eggs on but one of both sides and the hams fried. So he go to cook it himself.

[Loud shouts and wild laughter from the street. HORACE, ALMERIC, and LADY CREECH set their papers down in their laps and turn toward the door.]

MARIANO

Ha! He return from the kitchen with those national dish.

ETHEL

[glancing in the doorway]

How horrid!

[MICHELE backs out on the stoop from the doorway laughing, carrying a platter of ham and eggs.]

MICHELE

He have gone to wash himself at the street fountain.

[Tumult outside reaches its height, the shouts of "Yanka Dooda!" predominating.]

VASILI

[laughing, clapping his hands]

Bravo! Bravo!

ETHEL

Horrible!

[PIKE enters from the hotel. He is a youthful-looking American of about thirty-five, good-natured, shrewd, humorous, and kindly. His voice has the homely quality of the Central States, clear, quiet, and strong, with a very slight drawl at times when the situation strikes him as humorous, often exhibiting an apologetic character. He does not speak a dialect. His English is the United States language as spoken by the average citizen to be met on a daycoach anywhere in the Central States. He is clean-shaven, and his hair, which shows a slight tendency to gray, is neatly parted on the left side. His light straw hat is edged with a strip of ribbon. The hat, like the rest of his apparel, is neither new nor old. His shirt, "lay-down" collar, and cuffs are of white, well-laundered linen. He wears a loosely knotted tie. A linen motor-duster extends to his knees. His waistcoat is of a gray mixture, neither dark nor light. His trousers are of the same material and not fashionably cut, yet they fit him well and are neither baggy at the knees nor "high-water." His shoes are plain black Congress gaiters and show a "good shine." In brief, he is just the average well-to-do but untravelled citizen that you might meet on an accommodation train between Logansport and Kokomo, Indiana. As he enters he is wiping his face, after his ablutions, with a large towel, his hat pushed far back on his head. The sleeves of his duster are turned back, and his detachable cuffs are in his pocket. He comes through the doors rubbing his face with the towel, but, pausing for a moment on the stoop, drops the towel from his face to dry his hands. All except VASILI and the waiters stare at him with frowns of annoyance.]

PIKE

[beamingly unconscious of this, surprised, and in a tone of cheerful apology, believing all the world to be as good-natured and sensible as Kokomo would be under the circumstances]

Law! I didn't know there was folks here. I reckon you'll have to excuse me.

[As he speaks he dries his hands quickly.]

Here, son!

[He hands the towel to MICHELE. PIKE rapidly descends the steps, goes to the breakfast-table, joining VASILI and taking the seat opposite him.]

VASILI

[gayly]

You're a true patriot, my friend. You allow no profane hand to cook your national dish. I trust you will be as successful with that wicked motor of mine.

PIKE

[chuckling]

Lord bless your soul, I've put a self-binder together after a pony-engine had butted it half-way through a brick deepoe!

[Tucks his napkin in collar of his waistcoat and applies himself to the meal.]

[HORACE and HAWCASTLE read their papers, now and then casting glances of great annoyance at PIKE.]

[LADY CREECH lets her periodical rest in her lap, and without any abating or concealment, fixes PIKE with a basilisk glare which continues. He is unconscious of all this, his back being three-quarters to their group.]

VASILI

[no pause]

You have studied mechanics at the University?

PIKE

[smiling]

University? Law, no! On the old man's farm.

[VASILI nods gravely.]

HAWCASTLE

[blandly, to HORACE]

Without any disrespect to you, my dear fellow, what terrific bounders most of your fellow-countrymen are!

HORACE

[greatly irritated]

Do you wonder sis and I have emancipated ourselves?

39

HAWCASTLE

Not at all, my dear lad.

VASILI

[to PIKE]

Can I persuade you to accept a little of one of my own national dishes—caviar?

PIKE

Caviar? I've heard of it. I thought it was Rooshian.

VASILI

[disturbed, but instantly recovering, himself]

It is German, also. Will you not?

[He motions MARIANO to serve PIKE. MARIANO places a spoonful of caviar on a silver dish at PIKE'S right.]

PIKE

I expect I'd never get to the legislature again if the boys heard about it. Still, I reckon I'm far enough from home to take a *few* risks.

[He loads a fork with caviar, and with a smile places it in his mouth. The smile slowly fades, his face becomes thoughtful, then grave; he slowly sets the fork upon his plate, his eyes turn toward VASILI with a look both puzzled and plaintive, his mouth firmly closed, his jaw moving slightly.]

VASILI

I fear you do not like it. A few swallows of vodka will take away the taste.

[Gives him a glass, which PIKE accepts, drinking a mouthful in haste, VASILI watching him, sincerely concerned and troubled. PIKE swallows the vodka, quietly sets the glass down on the table, his eyelids begin to flutter, he bends a look of suffering and distrust upon VASILI, slowly rises and closes his eyes, then slowly sits and opens them. Gradually a faint, distrustful smile appears on his face.]

PIKE

[in the voice of a convalescent]

I never had any business to leave Indiana!

VASILI

I am sorry, my friend.

[PIKE takes another large forkful of caviar.]

VASILI

[observing this]

But I thought you did not like the caviar?

PIKE

It's to take away the taste of the vodka.

VASILI

[laughing]

I lift my hat to you.

PIKE

You never worked on a farm in your own country, Doc?

VASILI

That has been denied me.

PIKE

I expect so. Talk about things to drink! Harvest-time, and the women folks coming out from the house with a two-gallon jug of ice-cold buttermilk!

[Sets down the glass and whistles softly with delight.]

[HORACE shows increasing signs of annoyance.]

VASILI

You still enjoy those delights?

PIKE

Not since I moved up to our county-seat ten years ago and began to practice law. Things don't taste the same in the city.

VASILI

You do not like your city?

PIKE

[not with braggadocio, but earnestly, almost pathetically]

Like it? Well, sir, for public buildings and architecture, I wouldn't trade our State insane asylum for the worst-ruined ruin in Europe—not for hygiene and real comfort.

VASILI

And your people?

PIKE

The best on earth. Out *my* way folks are neighbors.

[HORACE snaps his paper sharply.]

VASILI

But you have no leisure class.

[VASILI is looking keenly at HAWCASTLE and HORACE as he speaks.]

PIKE

Got a pretty good-sized colored population.

VASILI

I mean no aristocracy—no great old families such as we have, that go back and back to the Middle Ages.

PIKE

[genially]

Well, I expect if they go back that far they might just as well set down and stay there. No, sir, the poor in my country don't have to pay taxes for a lot of useless kings and earls and first grooms of the bedchamber and second ladies in waiting, and I don't know what all. If anybody wants *our* money for nothin' he has to show energy enough to steal it. I wonder a man like you doesn't emigrate.

VASILI

Bravo!

HAWCASTLE

[to HORACE]

Your countryman seems to be rather down on us!

HORACE

This fellow is distinctly of the lower orders. We should cut him as completely in the States as here.

VASILI

I wonder you make this long journey, my friend, instead of to spend your holiday at home.

PIKE

Holiday! Why, *I* never had time even to go to Niagara Falls!

VASILI

[to MARIANO]

Finito!

[Sets his napkin carelessly on table and lights a Russian cigarette.]

MADAME DE CHAMPIGNY

What is it he does with his serviette?

PIKE

[moving his chair back from the table slightly, and folding his napkin]

43

No, *sir*, you wouldn't catch me puttin' in any time in these old kingdoms unless I had to.

LADY CREECH

[loudly, to HAWCASTLE]

Hawcastle, can you tell me how much longer these persons intend to remain here listening to our conversation?

[PIKE half turns to LADY CREECH, innocently puzzled.]

HAWCASTLE

Oh, it isn't that; but it's somewhat annoying not to be allowed to read one's paper in peace.

HORACE

Quite beastly annoying!

LADY CREECH

I had a distinct impression that the management had reserved this terrace for our party.

VASILI

[quietly]

I fear we have disturbed these good people.

PIKE

[in wonder]

Do you think they're hinting at us?

VASILI

I fear so.

PIKE

[gently and with sincere amazement]

Why, *we* haven't done anything to 'em.

44

VASILI

No, my friend.

PIKE

[smiling]

Well, I guess there ain't any bones broken.

HORACE

[throws down paper angrily on tea-table]
I can't stand this. I shall go for a stroll.

PIKE

[rising]

I expect it's about time for me to go and find the two young folks I've come to look after.

VASILI

You are here for a duty, then?

PIKE

[with gravity, yet smiling faintly]

I shouldn't be surprised if that was the name for it. Yes, sir, all the way from Indiana.

[ETHEL utters a low cry of fear.]

[HORACE, having secured his hat, is just rising to go, drops back into his chair with a stifled exclamation of dismay.]

[HAWCASTLE lays his paper flat on table. All this instantaneous.]

HAWCASTLE

By Jove!

[They all stare at PIKE.]

PIKE

[continuing]

I expect, prob'ly, Doc, I won't be able to eat with you this evening. You see—

[he pauses, somewhat embarrassed]

—you see, I've come a mighty long ways to look after her, and she, prob'ly—that is, *they'll* prob'ly want me to have supper with *them*.

[The latter part of this speech is spoken rather breathlessly, though not rapidly, and almost tremulously, and with a growing smile that is like a confession.]

VASILI

Do not trouble for me. Your young people, they have a villa?

PIKE

No; they're right here in this hotel.

HORACE

I must get away!

[He says this huskily, almost in a whisper, as if to himself. His face is tense with anxiety.]

VASILI

[with a gesture of dismissal, though graciously]

Seek them. I finish my cigarette.

PIKE

Guess I better ask.

[HORACE is crossing, meaning to get away through the grove.]

PIKE

[addressing him]

Hey, there! Can you—

46

[HORACE, proceeding, pays no attention.]

PIKE

[lifting his voice]

Excuse me, son, ain't you an American?

[More decidedly, to MARIANO.]

Waiter, tell that gentleman I'm speaking to him.

MARIANO

[to HORACE]

M'sieu', that gentleman speak with you.

HORACE

[agitated and angry]

What gentleman?

[MARIANO bows toward PIKE.]

PIKE

[at same time genially]

I thought from your looks you must be an American.

HORACE

[turning haughtily]

Are you speaking to *me*?

PIKE

[good-humoredly]

Well, I shouldn't be surprised. Ain't you an American?

HORACE

I happen to have been born in the States.

47

PIKE

[amiably]

Well, that *was* luck!

HORACE

[turning as if to go]

Will you kindly excuse me?

PIKE

Hold on a minute! I'm looking for some Americans here, and I expect you know 'em—boy and girl named Simpson.

HORACE

Is there any possibility that you mean Granger-Simpson?

[His tone is both alarmed and truculent.]

PIKE

[much pleased]

No, sir; just plain Simpson. Granger's their middle name. That's for old Jed Granger, grandfather on their ma's side.

[He pronounces "ma" with the broad Hoosier accent—"maw."]

I want to see 'em both, but it's the girl I'm rilly looking for.

HORACE

[trembling, but speaking even more haughtily]

Will you be good enough to state any possible reason why Miss Granger-Simpson should see you?

PIKE

[in profound surprise, yet mildly]

Reason—why, yes—I'm her guardian.

[ETHEL lifts her hand to her forehead as if dizzy. MADAME DE

48

CHAMPIGNY puts an arm around her. ETHEL recovers herself and stands rigidly, staring at PIKE.]

HORACE

[staggered]

What!

PIKE

[smiling]

Yes, sir, Daniel Voorhees Pike, attorney at law, Kokomo, Indiana.

[HORACE falls back from him in horror.]

[HAWCASTLE, excited but cool, makes a quick, imperative gesture to LADY CREECH, who majestically sweeps up to ETHEL, kisses her on the forehead in lofty pity, and sweeps out.]

[MADAME DE CHAMPIGNY kisses ETHEL compassionately on cheek and follows LADY CREECH off.]

[MARIANO and MICHELE, having cleared the table, exeunt.]

HORACE

[hoarse with shame, to PIKE; slight pause after PIKE'S last speech.]

I shall ask her if she will consent to an interview.

PIKE

[at same time, astounded]

"Consent to an interview"? Why, I want to *talk* to her!

HAWCASTLE

[quickly and earnestly to ETHEL]

This shall make no difference to *us*, my child. Speak to him at once.

[Exit into the hotel.]

49

PIKE

[to HORACE]

Don't you understand? I'm her *guardian.*

HORACE

[with a desperate gesture]

I shall never hold up my head again!

[Rushes off.]

VASILI

[gravely, to PIKE]

When you have finished your affairs, my friend, remember my poor car yonder.

PIKE

[with a melancholy smile]

All right, Doc, I'm kind of confused just now, but I reckon I can still put a plug back in a gear-box.

VASILI

[at same time]

Then *au revoir*, my friend.

[Strolls off through the grove.]

PIKE

[watching him go, thoughtfully]

Yes, *sir*!

ETHEL

[haughtily, yet with the air of confessing a humiliating truth, her eyes cast down]

I am Miss Granger-Simpson.

[As she speaks he turns and lifts his hand toward her as if suddenly startled. He has not seen her until now. He stands for a moment in silence, looking at her with great tenderness and pride.]

PIKE

[with both wonder and pathos in his voice]

Why, I knew your pa from the time I was a little boy till he died, and I looked up to him more'n I ever looked up to anybody in my life, but I never thought he'd have a girl like you!

[She turns from him; he takes a short step nearer her.]

He'd 'a' been mighty proud if he could see you now.

ETHEL

[quickly, and with controlled agitation]

Perhaps it will be as well if we avoid personal allusions.

PIKE

[mildly]

I don't see how that's possible.

ETHEL

[sitting]

Will you please sit down?

PIKE

Yes, ma'am!

[ETHEL shivers at the "ma'am."]

[He sits in the chair which HORACE has occupied, still holding his hat in his hand.]

ETHEL

[tremulously, her eyes cast down]

As you know, I—I—

[She stops, as if afraid of breaking down; then, turning toward him, cries sharply.]

Oh, are you *really* my guardian?

PIKE

[smiling]

Well, I've got the papers in my grip. I expect—

ETHEL

Oh, I KNOW it! It is only that we didn't fancy, we didn't expect—

PIKE

I expect you thought I'd be considerable older.

ETHEL

Not only *that*—

PIKE

[interrupting gently]

I expect you thought I'd neglected you a good deal,

[remorsefully]

and it *did* LOOK like it—never comin' to see you; but I couldn't hardly manage the time to get away. You see, bein' trustee of your share of the estate, I don't hardly have a fair show at my law practice. But when I got your letter, eleven days ago, I says to myself: "Here, Daniel Voorhees Pike, you old shellback, you've just got to *take* time. John Simpson trusted you with his property, and he's done more

[his voice rises, but his tone is affectionate and shows deep feeling]

—he's trusted you to look out for *her*, and now she's come to a kind of jumpin'-off place in her life—she's thinking of gettin' married; and you just pack your grip-sack and hike out over there and stand *by* her!"

52

ETHEL

[frigidly]

I quite fail to understand your point of view. Perhaps I had best make it at once clear to you that I am no longer *thinking* of marrying.

PIKE

[leaning back in his chair and smiling on her]

Well, Lord-a-Mercy!

ETHEL

I mean I have decided upon it. The ceremony is to take place within a fortnight.

PIKE

Well, I declare!

ETHEL

We shall dispense with all delays.

PIKE

[slowly and a little sadly]

Well, I don't know as I could rightly say anything against that. He must be a mighty nice fellow, and you must think a heap *of* him!

[With a suppressed sigh.]

That's the way it should be.

[He smiles again and leans toward her in a friendly way.]

And you're happy, are you?

ETHEL

[with cold emphasis, sitting very straight in her chair]

Distinctly!

[PIKE'S expression becomes puzzled, he passes his hand over his chin, looks at her keenly. Then his eyes turn to the spot where HORACE stood during their interview, and he starts, as though shocked at a sudden thought.]

PIKE

It ain't that fellow I was talkin' to yonder?

ETHEL

[indignantly]

That was my *brother*!

PIKE

[relieved, but somewhat embarrassed]

Lord-a-Mercy!

[Recovering himself immediately and smiling.]

But, naturally, I wouldn't remember him. He couldn't have been more than twelve years old last time you were home. Of course, I'd 'a' known *you*—

ETHEL

How? You couldn't have seen me since I was a child.

PIKE

From your picture. Though now I see—it *ain't* so much like you.

ETHEL

You have a photograph of *me*?

PIKE

[very gently]

The last time I saw your father alive he gave me one.

ETHEL

[frowning]

Gave it to you?

54

PIKE

Gave it to me to look at.

ETHEL

And you remembered—

PIKE

[apologetically]

Yes, ma'am!

ETHEL

[incredulously]

Remembered well enough to *know* me?

PIKE

Yes, ma'am!

ETHEL

It does not strike me as possible. We may dismiss the subject.

PIKE

Well, if you'd like to introduce me to your

[laughing feebly and tentatively, hesitates]

—to your—

ETHEL

To my brother?

PIKE

No, ma'am; I mean to your—to the young man.

ETHEL

To Mr. St. Aubyn? I think it quite unnecessary.

55

PIKE

I'm afraid I can't see it just that way

[with an apologetic laugh]

I'll *have* to have a couple of talks with him—sort of look him over, so to speak. I won't stay around here spoilin' your fun any longer than I can help. Only just for that, and to get a letter I'm expectin' here from England. Don't you be afraid.

ETHEL

I do not see that you need have come at all.

[Her lip begins to tremble.]

We could have been spared this mortification.

PIKE

[sadly]

You mean *I* mortify you? Why, I—I can't see how.

ETHEL

In a hundred ways—every way. That common person who is with you—

PIKE

[gently]

He ain't common. You only think so because he's with *me*.

ETHEL

[sharply]

Who is he?

PIKE

He told me his name, but I can't remember it. I call him "Doc."

56

ETHEL

It doesn't *matter*! What *does* matter is that you needn't have come. You could have *written* your consent.

PIKE

[mildly]

Not without seeing the young man.

ETHEL

And you could have arranged the settlement in the same way.

PIKE

[smiling]

Settlement? You seem to have *settled* it pretty well without me.

ETHEL

You do not understand. An alliance of this sort always entails a certain settlement.

PIKE

Yes, ma'am—when folks get married they generally settle down considerable.

ETHEL

[impatiently]

Please listen. If you were at all a man of the world, I should not have to explain that in marrying into a noble house I bring my *dot*, my dowry—

PIKE

[puzzled]

Money, you mean?

ETHEL

If you choose to put it that way.

PIKE

You mean you want to put aside something of your own to buy a lot and fix up a place to start housekeeping—

ETHEL

No, *no*! I mean a settlement upon Mr. St. Aubyn directly.

PIKE

You mean you want to *give* it to him?

ETHEL

If that's the only way to make you understand—*yes*!

PIKE

[amused]

How much do you want to give him?

ETHEL

[coldly]

A hundred and fifty thousand pounds.

PIKE

[incredulously]

Seven hundred and fifty thousand dollars!

ETHEL

Precisely that!

PIKE

[amazed]

Well, he *has* made you care for him! I guess he must be the Prince of the World, honey! He must be a great man. I expect you're right about me not meetin' *him*! I prob'ly wouldn't stack up very high alongside of a man that's big enough for you to think as much of as you do of him.

58

[Smiling.]

Why, I'd have to squeeze every bit of property your pa left you.

ETHEL

Is it *your* property?

PIKE

[gently]

I've worked pretty hard to take care of it for you.

ETHEL

[rising impulsively and coming to him]

Forgive me for saying that.

PIKE

[smiling]

Pshaw!

ETHEL

It was unworthy of me, unworthy of the higher and nobler things that life calls me to live up to

[proudly]

—that I *shall* live up to. The money means nothing to me—I am not thinking of that. It is merely a necessary form.

PIKE

Have you talked with Mr. St. Aubyn about this settlement—this present you want to make him?

ETHEL

Not with him.

PIKE

[amused]

I thought not! You'll see—he wouldn't take it if I'd let you give it to him. A fine man like that wants to make his own way, of course. Mighty few men like to have fun poked at 'em about livin' on their wife's money.

ETHEL

[despairingly]

Oh, I *can't* make you understand! A settlement isn't a gift.

PIKE

[as if humoring her]

How'd you happen to decide that just a hundred and fifty thousand pounds was what you wanted to give him?

ETHEL

It was Mr. St. Aubyn's father who fixed the amount.

PIKE

His *father*? What's *he* got to do with it?

ETHEL

He is the Earl of Hawcastle, the head of the ancient house.

PIKE

And he asks you for your property—asks you for it in so many words?

ETHEL

As a *settlement*!

PIKE

[aghast]

And your young man *knows* it?

ETHEL

I tell you I have not discussed it with Mr. St. Aubyn.

PIKE

[emphatically]

I reckon not! Well, sir, do you know what's the first thing Mr. St. Aubyn will do when he hears his father's made such a proposition to you? He'll take the old man out in the back lot and give him a thrashing he won't forget to the day of his death!

[The roll of drums is heard, distant, as if sounding below the cliff; bugle sounds at the same time.]

[MARIANO and MICHELE run hurriedly from the hotel and lean over balustrade at back, as if watching something below the cliff.]

[RIBIERE enters quickly with them, takes one quick glance in same direction, and hurries off.]

[PIKE and ETHEL, surprised, turn to look.]

MARIANO

[calling to ETHEL as he enters]

A bandit of Russia, Mademoiselle! The soldiers think he hide in a grotto under the cliff!

[ALMERIC comes on rapidly from the hotel, carrying a shot-gun.]

ALMERIC

[enthusiastically, as he enters]

Oh, I *say*, fair sport, by Jove! Fair sport!

PIKE

[to ETHEL, indicating ALMERIC, chuckling]

I saw *him* on the road here—what's he meant for?

ALMERIC

Think I'll have a chance to pot the beggar, Michele?

[He joins MICHELE at balustrade.]

MICHELE

No, Signore, there are two companies of carabiniere.

[PIKE, delighted, chuckles aloud.]

ETHEL

[angry, calling]

Almeric!

ALMERIC

[turning]

Hallo!

ETHEL

[frigidly]

I wish to present my guardian to you.

[To PIKE.]

This is Mr. St. Aubyn.

ALMERIC

[coming down]

Hallo, though! It's the donkey man, isn't it? How very odd! You'll have to see the Governor and our solicitor about the settlement. I've some important business here. The police are chasing a bally convict chap under the cliffs over yonder, so you'll have to excuse me. I'll have to be toddling.

[Goes up to terrace wall overlooking cliffs.]

You know there's nothing like a little convict shooting to break the blooming monotony—what?

[The bugle sounds. ALMERIC turns and rushes off.]

Wait for me, you fellows! Don't hurt him till *I* get there!

[His voice dies away in the distance.]

PIKE

[turning to ETHEL with slow horror]

Seven hundred and fifty thousand dollars for—How much do they charge over here for a *real* man?

[She is unable to meet his eye. She turns, with flaming cheeks, and runs into the hotel. He stands staring after her, incredulous, dumfounded, in a frozen attitude.]

END OF THE FIRST ACT

63

THE SECOND ACT

Scene: Entrance garden of the hotel.

In the distance are seen the green slopes of vineyards, a ruined castle, and olive orchards leading up the mountainside.

An old stone wall seven feet high runs across the rear of the stage. This wall is almost covered with vines, showing autumn tints, crowning the crest of the wall and hanging from it in profusion. There is a broad green gate of the Southern Italian type, closed. A white-columned pergola runs obliquely down from the wall on the right. The top of the pergola is an awning formed by a skeleton of green-painted wooden strips thickly covered by entwining lemon branches bearing ripening lemons. Between the columns of the pergola are glimpses of a formal Italian garden: flowers, hedges, and a broad flat marble vase on a slender pedestal, etc. On the left a two-story wing of the hotel meets the wall at the back and runs square across to the left; a lemon grove lies to the left also. The wall of the hotel facing the audience shows open double doors, with windows up-stairs and below, all with lowered awnings. There is a marble bench at the left among shrubberies; an open touring-car upon the right under the awning formed by the overhang of the pergola; a bag of tools, open, on the stage near by, the floor boards of the car removed, the apron lifted.

As the curtain rises, PIKE, in his shirt-sleeves, his hands dirty, and wearing a workman's long blouse buttoned at neck, is bending over the engine, working and singing, at intervals whistling "The Blue and the Gray." His hat, duster, and cuffs are on the rear seat of the tonneau.

[Enter HORACE from the garden. He is flushed and angry; controls himself with an effort, trying to speak politely.]

HORACE

Mr. Pike!

PIKE

[apparently not hearing him, hammering at a bolt-head with a monkey-wrench and singing]

64

"One lies down at Appomattox—"

HORACE

[sharply]

Mr. Pike! Mr. Pike, I wish a word with you.

PIKE

[looks up mildly]

Hum!

[He moves to the other side of the engine, rubbing handle of monkey-wrench across his chin as if puzzled.]

HORACE

I wish to tell you that the surprise of this morning so upset me that I went for a long walk. I have just returned.

PIKE

[regarding the machine intently, sings softly]

"One wore clothes of gray—."

[Then he whistles the air. Throughout this interview he maintains almost constantly an air of absorption in his work and continues to whistle and sing softly.]

HORACE

[continuing]

I have been even more upset by what I have just learned from my sister.

PIKE

[absently]

Why, that's too bad.

HORACE

It *is* too bad—absurdly—monstrously bad! She tells me that she has done you the honor to present you to the family with which we are forming an alliance—to the Earl of Hawcastle—her fiancé's father—

PIKE

[with cheerful absent-mindedness—working]

Yes, sir!

HORACE

[continuing]

To her fiancé's aunt, Lady Creech—

PIKE

Yes, sir! the whole possetucky of them.

[Singing softly.]

"She was my hanky-panky-danky from the town of Kalamazack!" Yes, sir—that French lady, too.

[He throws a quick, keen glance at HORACE, then instantly appears absorbed in work again, singing,]

"She ran away with a circus clown—she never did come back—Oh, Solomon Levi!"

[Continues to whistle the tune softly.]

HORACE

And she introduced you to her fiancé—to Mr. St. Aubyn himself.

PIKE

[looking up, monkey-wrench in hand]

Yes, sir;

[chuckles]

we had quite a talk about shootin' in Indiana; said he'd heard of Peru, in his school history. Wanted to come out some day, he said, and asked what our best game was. I told him we had some Incas

66

still preserved in the mountains of Indiana, and he said he'd like a good Inca head to put up in his gun-room. He *ought* to get one, *oughtn't* he?

[Starts to work again, busily.]

HORACE

[indignantly]

My sister informs me that in spite of Lord Hawcastle's most graciously offering to discuss her engagement with you, you refused.

PIKE

Well, I didn't see any need of it.

HORACE

Furthermore, you allege that you will decline to go into the matter with Lord Hawcastle's solicitor.

PIKE

What matter?

HORACE

[angrily]

The matter of the settlement.

PIKE

[quietly]

Your sister kind of let it out to me awhile ago that you think a good deal of this French widow lady. Suppose you make up your mind to take her for richer or poorer—what's *she* going to give *you*?

HORACE

[roaring]

Nothing! What do you mean?

67

PIKE

Well, I thought you'd probably charge her

[with a slight drawl]

a *little*, anyhow. Ain't that the way over here?

[Turns to work again, humming "Dolly Gray."]

HORACE

It is impossible for you to understand the motives of my sister and myself in our struggle *not* to remain in the vulgar herd. But can't you try to comprehend that there is an Old-World society, based not on wealth, but on that indescribable something which comes of ancient lineage and high birth?

[With great indignation.]

You presume to interfere between us and the fine flower of Europe!

PIKE

[straightening up, but speaking quietly]

Well, I don't know as the folks around Kokomo would ever have spoke of your father as a "fine flower," but we thought a heap of him, and when he married your ma he was so glad to get her—well, I never heard yet that he asked for any *settlement*!

HORACE

You are quite impossible.

PIKE

The fact is, when she took him he was a poor man; but if he'd a had seven hundred and fifty thousand dollars, I'll bet he'd 'a' given it for her.

[Starts to hammer vigorously, humming "Dolly Gray."]

HORACE

There is no profit in continuing the discussion.

[Turns on his heel, but immediately turns again toward PIKE, who is apparently preoccupied.]

And I warn you we shall act without paying the slightest attention to you.

[Triumphantly.]

What have you to say to that, sir?

[PIKE'S answer is conveyed by the motor-horn, which says: "Honk! Honk!" HORACE throws up his hands despairingly. PIKE'S voice becomes audible in the last words of the song: "Good-bye, Dolly Gray."]

[Enter LADY CREECH and ALMERIC through the gates.]

HORACE

[meeting them]

The fellow is hopeless.

LADY CREECH

[not hearing, and speaking from habit, automatically]

Dreadful person!

[PIKE continues his work, paying no attention.]

ALMERIC

[to HORACE]

Better let him alone till the Governor's had time to think a bit. Governor's clever. He'll fetch the beggar about somehow.

LADY CREECH

[with a Parthian glance at the unconscious PIKE]

I sha'h't stop in the creature's presence—I shall go up to my room for my forty winks.

[Exit into the hotel.]

ALMERIC

[as she goes out]

Day-day, aunt!

[To HORACE]

I'm off to look at that pup again. You trust the Governor.

HORACE

[as ALMERIC goes]

I do, I do. It is insufferable, but I'll wait.

[Exit into the garden.]

[PIKE stands for a moment, contemplating the car in some despondency, still humming or whistling.]

[LADY CREECH, after a few moments, appears at a window in the upper story of the hotel. Unseen by PIKE, she pulls up the awning for a better view, and drops lace curtains inside of window so as to screen herself from observation. Sits watching.]

[Immediately upon HORACE'S exit MARIANO, flustered, enters hurriedly from the hotel, goes to the gates, and fumbles with the lock. At the same time VASILI enters from the garden, smoking.]

VASILI

You make progress, my friend?

PIKE

Your machine's like a good many people—got sand in its gear-box.

VASILI

[to MARIANO]

Are you locking us in?

MARIANO

[excitedly coming down and showing a big key which he has taken from the lock]

70

No, Herr von Gröllerhagen, I lock some one *out*—that bandit who have not been capture. The carabiniere warn us to close all gates for an hour. They will have that wicked one soon. There are two companies.

[In a lower tone to VASILI.]

Monsieur Ribiere has much fears.

VASILI

Monsieur Ribiere is sometimes a fool.

MARIANO

[in a hoarse whisper]

Monsieur, this convict is a Russian.

[VASILI waves him away somewhat curtly.]

[Exit MARIANO, shaking his head, carrying the key with him.]

PIKE

Two companies of soldiers! A town marshal out my way would 'a' had him yesterday.

VASILI

My friend, you are teaching me to respect your country, not by what you brag, but by what you do.

PIKE

How's that.

VASILI

[significantly]

I see how a son of that great democracy can apply himself to a dirty machine, while his eyes are full of visions of one of its beautiful daughters.

PIKE

[slowly and sadly, peering into the machine]

Doc, there's sand in your gear-box.

VASILI

[laughing]

So?

PIKE

You go down to the kitchen and make signs for some of the help to give you a nice clean bunch of rags.

VASILI

[surprised into hauteur]

What is it you ask me to do?

PIKE

I need some more rags.

VASILI

[amused]

My friend, I obey.

[Makes a mock-serious bow and starts.]

PIKE

I won't leave the machine—'twouldn't be safe.

VASILI

[halting, laughs]

You fear this famous bandit would steal it?

PIKE

No; but there's parties around here might think it was a settlement.

VASILI

I do not understand.

PIKE

[chuckling]

Doc, that's where we're in the same fix.

VASILI

Weidersehn, my friend.

[Exit into hotel.]

[PIKE kneels on the foot-board of machine above gear-box, begins to clean, using an old rag, singing "Sweet Genevieve." A distant shot is heard. PIKE looks up at this, ceasing to sing. Then he continues his work and music. LADY CREECH leans out from her window, staring off to the right with opera-glasses. There is a noise at the gates as some one hastily but cautiously tries to open them. PIKE looks up again, turns toward the gates, and, after a short pause, again begins to sing and work, but very softly.]

[IVANOFF appears on top of the wall at back, climbing up cautiously from lane below. He creeps from the wall to the top of pergola and cautiously along that through the foliage to above PIKE. He peers over the foliage at PIKE.]

[PIKE looks up slowly, and, as slowly, stops "Sweet Genevieve," his voice fading away on a half syllable as he encounters IVANOFF'S gaze. They stare at each other, LADY CREECH observing unseen.]

[IVANOFF is a thin, very fragile-looking man of thirty-eight. His disordered hair is prematurely gray, his beard is a grizzled four days' stubble. He is exceedingly haggard and worn, but has the face and look of a man of refinement and cultivation. He has lost his hat; his shoes and trousers are splashed with dried mud, and brambles cling to him here and there. He wears a soiled white shirt and collar, and a torn black tie, black waistcoat and trousers. He is covered with dust from head to foot; one sleeve of his shirt has been torn off at the elbow. He wears no coat.]

IVANOFF

[in a voice tremulous with tragic appeal]

Et ce que vous êtes un homme de bon coeur? Je ne suis pas coupable—

73

PIKE

[very gravely]

There ain't any use in the world your talkin' to me like that!

IVANOFF

[panting]

You are an Englishman?

PIKE

[quietly, rising and stepping back]

That'll do for *that*. You come down from there!

IVANOFF

[in a voice that lifts, almost cracks, with sudden hope]
An American?

PIKE

They haven't made me anything else yet.

IVANOFF

[swinging himself down to the ground]

Thank God for that!

[He leans against the car, exhausted.]

PIKE

I do. What makes *you* so glad about it?

IVANOFF

Because I have suffered in the cause your own forefathers gave their lives for. I am a Russian political fugitive, and I can go no farther. If you give me up I shall not be taken alive. I have no weapon, but I can find a way to cut my throat.

74

PIKE

[with humorous incredulity]

Are *you* the bandit they're lookin' for?

IVANOFF

They call me that. Do I look like a bandit?

PIKE

How close are they?

IVANOFF

[with despairing gesture]

There!

PIKE

Did they see you climb that wall?

IVANOFF

I think not.

[There comes a loud ringing at the gates. At the sound IVANOFF starts violently, throwing one arm up as if to shield his face from a blow.]

IVANOFF

Oh, my God! it is they!

[He staggers back against the machine.]

PIKE

[hastily stripping off his working blouse]

Do you know anything about gear-box plugs?

[The ringing continues.]

IVANOFF

Nothing in the world.

PIKE

Then you're a chauffeur.

[Puts blouse on him.]

Take a look at this one.

[With emphatic significance.]

It's *underneath* the machine.

[Quickly sets his hands on IVANOFF'S shoulders, having forced the blouse on him, and pushes him beneath the car.]

MARIANO

[within the hotel, calling]

Subito! Subito! Vengo, Signore! Vengo!

[PIKE at same time rapidly wipes his hands on a rag, puts on his hat, cuffs, and coat, which have been lying on the seat.]

MARIANO

[running on, flustered]

Corpo de St. Costanzo! Non posso essere dapertutto allo stesso tempo. Vengo, vengo!

[He hastens to the gates with his key, unfastening busily. Meanwhile PIKE lights a cigar.]

MARIANO

Ecco!

[Throws open gates and falls back in astonishment.]

Dio mio!

[Two carabiniere, good-looking, soldierly men in the carabiniere uniform, cocked hats, white cross-belts, etc., are disclosed, their carbines slung over their arms, their long cloaks thrown back. Behind the carabiniere stand some fishermen in red caps, dirty flannel shirts, and trousers rolled up to the knee; also a few ragged beggars.]

76

FIRST CARABINIERE

[as gate is opened]

Buon giorno!

[The two carabiniere enter briskly.]

MARIANO

[springing forward and closing gate, calling to crowd outside]

No, no!

FIRST CARABINIERE

Ceerchimo l'assassino Russo.

MARIANO

Dio mio! Non nell' Albergo Regina Margherita.

SECOND CARABINIERE

[coming to PIKE]

Avete visto un uomo scavalcare il muro?

PIKE

[genially]

Wishing you many happy returns, Colonel!

MARIANO

[greatly excited]

It is the robber of Russia. They think he climb the wall, the assassin. The other carabiniere, they surround all yonder.

[Gesturing right and left.]

These two they search here. They ask you, please, have you see him climb the wall.

PIKE

No.

FIRST CARABINIERE

Ae quelcuno passato de qui?

MARIANO

He say has any one go across here?

PIKE

No.

FIRST CARABINIERE

[pointing under the car]

Chi costui?

MARIANO

He want to know who that is.

PIKE

The new chauffeur for the machine, from Naples.

MARIANO

E lo chauffeur di un illustre personaggio padrone dell' automobile.

FIRST CARABINIERE

[bowing to PIKE]

Grazia, Signore.

[To MARIANO.]

Cerchereremo nel giardino.

[Exit swiftly FIRST CARABINIERE to the right through pergola; SECOND to the left.]

MARIANO

Dio mio! but those are the brave men, Signore. Either one shall meet in a moment this powerful assassin who may take his lifes.

[Murmur of voice from back arises, sounds of running feet and shrill whistles and pounding on gates.]

[MARIANO runs back, opens the gates, showing excited and clamoring fishermen and beggars in the lane. They try to come in. He drives them back with a napkin, which has been hanging over his arm, crying: "Vate, vate! Devo dire al maresciallo di cacciarvi?"]

[Meanwhile VASILI has entered from the hotel, a bundle of clean white rags in his hand.]

VASILI

Is there a new eruption of Vesuvius?

PIKE

[meeting him and taking the rags]

No; it's an eruption of colonels trying to arrest a high-school professor. I've got him under your car there.

VASILI

[astounded]

What!

PIKE

I told them he's your new chauffeur.

VASILI

My friend, do you realize the penalty for protecting a criminal from arrest?

PIKE

We'll be proud of the risk.

[Speaks in an undertone to IVANOFF.]

This man owns the car. You can trust him the same as your own father.

VASILI

[remonstrating]

79

My friend, my friend!

PIKE

[quietly]

Look out, the Governor's staff is coming back.

MARIANO

[closing the gates and wiping his face]

Lazzaroni!

[At the same time FIRST CARABINIERE enters from right; SECOND CARABINIERE from left.]

SECOND CARABINIERE

Niente!

FIRST CARABINIERE

Niente la!

[The two CARABINIERE cross briskly to each other as they speak, and stand conferring.]

MARIANO

Grazia Dio! He has gone some other place!

PIKE

[very casually to VASILI]

You'll have to get a new off front tire, Doc. That one is pretty near gone. Better have Jim, here, put on the spare when he gets through.

[The CARABINIERE beckon to MARIANO and speak to him.]

VASILI

[seriously, stepping toward PIKE]

Do you know what you are asking me to do?

PIKE

[watching CARABINIERE]

To put on a new tire.

[VASILI, with exclamation and gesture of despair grimly tinged with humor, turns away, greatly disturbed.]

MARIANO

[addressing PIKE with an embarrassed bow]

The carabiniere with all excuses beg if you will command the chauffeur to step forth from the automobile.

PIKE

No, sir; I worked on that machine myself for three hours. He's got his hands full of nuts and screws and bolts half fastened. If he lays them down now to come out I don't know how long it'll take to get them back in place. We want to get this job finished.

[Continues with a plaintive uplift of voice.]

This is *serious*! Tell them to go on up Main Street with their Knights of Pythias parade, and come around some day when we haven't got our hands full.

MARIANO

[meekly]

I tell them—yes, sir.

[Turns and confers with the CARABINIERE.]

PIKE

It'll be your turn in a minute, Doc; be mighty careful what you say.

MARIANO

Because the chauffeur have been engaged only to-day and have just arrived, the carabiniere ask ten thousand pardons, but inquire how long he have been known to his employer.

[He bows to VASILI with embarrassment.]

PIKE

How long? Why, he was raised on his father's farm.

[He faces VASILI, and stretches his arm out toward him as if for corroboration.]

MARIANO

[to VASILI]

Oh, if that is so!

PIKE

It *is* so; ain't it, Doc?

VASILI

[to. MARIANO, with dignity]

You have heard my friend say it.

MARIANO

[to VASILI, in a serious undertone]

Monseigneur graciously consents that I reveal his incognito to the carabiniere.

VASILI

Is it necessary?

MARIANO

Otherwise I fear they will not withdraw; they have suspicion.

VASILI

[with a gesture of resignation]

Very well, tell them. I rely upon them to preserve my incognito from all others.

MARIANO

[bowing deeply]

Monseigneur, they will be discreet.

[Goes up to CARABINIERE and speaks to them.]

PIKE

[aside to IVANOFF]

Make a noise—keep busy.

[Then with more emphasis.]

But don't you unscrew anything!

MARIANO

[to VASILI, smiling]

Monseigneur, they withdraw.

[The CARABINIERE, with great deference and gravity, salute VASILI. He returns the salute curtly.]

FIRST CARABINIERE. Mille grazias, Signore!

[MARIANO throws the gates open, the two CARABINIERE go rapidly out, sweeping the crowd away. MARIANO closes the gates.]

PIKE

[giving MARIANO a coin]

You're pretty good.

MARIANO

It required but the slightest diplomacy, Signore. Thank you, Signore!

[Exit into the hotel.]

PIKE

[puzzled]

He must have mesmerized the militia.

VASILI

[glancing off]

It is quite safe for the time.

PIKE

[going to the car]

It's all right, old man!

[Extends his hand to IVANOFF and helps him up from beneath the machine.]

IVANOFF

I will pray God for you all my life.

PIKE

Wait till we get you plumb out of the woods.

IVANOFF

[to VASILI]

And you, sir, if I could speak my gratitude—

VASILI

[crisply]

My American friend yonder has placed himself—and myself—in danger of the penal code of Italy for protecting you. Perhaps you will be so good as to let us know for what we have incriminated ourselves.

IVANOFF

[looking at him keenly]

You are a Russian?

PIKE

Don't be afraid—he's only a German.

IVANOFF

[bitterly]

The Italian journals call me a brigand, inspired by the Russian legation in Rome. My name is Ivanoff Ivanovitch.

PIKE

[reassuringly]

All right, old man!

IVANOFF

I was condemned in Petersburg ten years ago. I was a professor of the languages, a translator in the bureau of the Minister of Finance. I was a member of the Society of the Blue Fifty, a constitutionalist.

PIKE

Good for you.

IVANOFF

I was able to do little for the cause, though I tried.

VASILI

How did you try?

IVANOFF

I transferred funds of the government to the Society of the Blue Fifty. Never one ruble for myself.

[Strikes himself on the breast.]

It was for Russia's sake—not mine!

VASILI

[sharply]

But you committed the great Russian crime of getting yourself caught?

IVANOFF

Through treachery. There was an Englishman who lived in Petersburg. He had contracts with the government—I thought he was my best friend. I had married in my student days in Paris—ah, it is the old story!

[bitterly]

I knew that this Englishman admired my wife; but I trusted him—as I trusted her—and he made my house his home. I had fifty thousand rubles in my desk to be delivered to my society. The police came to search; they found only me—but not my wife nor my English friend—nor the fifty thousand rubles! I went to Siberia. Now I search for those two.

VASILI

[gravely]

Was it they who sent the police?

IVANOFF

After they had taken the money and were beyond the frontier themselves. That is all I have against them.

PIKE

[gently]

Looks to me like it would be enough.

VASILI

Then, by your own confession, you are an embezzler and a revolutionist.

PIKE

[going to VASILI quickly]

Why, the man's down; you wouldn't go back on him now.

[With a half chuckle.]

Besides, you've made yourself one of his confederates.

86

VASILI

Upon my soul, so I have.

[Bursts into laughter and lays his hands on PIKE'S shoulders.]

My friend, from my first sight of you in the hotel at Napoli I saw that you were a great man.

PIKE

[grinning]

What are you doing, running for Congress?

VASILI

[after a grave look at IVANOFF, turns to PIKE again]

I do not think that the carabiniere went away without suspicion.

IVANOFF

Suspicion! They will watch every exit from the hotel and its grounds. What can I do, until darkness—

PIKE

[motioning toward the hotel]

Why, Doc's got the whole lower floor of this wing—you're his chauffeur—

VASILI

[quickly, grimly]

I was about to suggest it. I have a room that can easily be spared to Professor Ivanoff.

IVANOFF

[going to them, greatly touched]

My friends, God bless both of you!

[As he speaks he shakes hands with PIKE and turns to offer his hand to VASILI, who, apparently without noticing it, goes up toward the hotel.]

PIKE

Don't waste time talkin' about that. I shouldn't be surprised if you were hungry.

[Takes him by elbow and walks him to door of hotel.]

IVANOFF

I have had no food for a day.

VASILI

[grimly]

My valet de chambre will attend to Professor Ivanoff's needs. No one shall be allowed to enter his room.

PIKE

And don't you go out of it, either.

VASILI

He shall not. This way.

[The three go into the hotel. Immediately on their disappearance LADY CREECH'S curtains are whisked aside; she pops out of the window with the suddenness of Punch, leans far out with her head upside down, at the risk of her neck, trying to watch them even after they have entered the hotel. Laughter of MADAME DE CHAMPIGNY heard at left. LADY CREECH waves her hand as if signalling in that direction and withdraws from window.]

[Enter HORACE and MADAME DE CHAMPIGNY from the garden, he carrying her parasol and looking into her eyes. She is laughing.]

[Enter LADY CREECH from the hotel, wildly excited.]

LADY CREECH

Have you seen my brother—where is Lord Hawcastle?

HORACE

On the other side of the hotel, Lady Creech; down there on the last terrace just as far as you can go.

[Exit LADY CREECH down left.]

HORACE

Ah, but you laugh at me, chere Comtesse!

MADAME DE CHAMPIGNY

[gently]

It is because I cannot believe you are always serious.

HORACE

Serious? Like a lady to her knight of old, set me some task to prove how serious I am.

[Deliriously.]

Anything!

MADAME DE CHAMPIGNY

Ah, gladly! Complete those odious settlement! Overcome the resistance of this bad man who so trouble your sweet sister!

HORACE

You promise me when it is settled that I may speak to you

[becomes suddenly nervous and embarrassed]

—that I may speak to you—

MADAME DE CHAMPIGNY

[sweetly]

Yes—speak to me—

HORACE

Speak as—as you must know I want to speak—as I hardly dare—

MADAME DE CHAMPIGNY

[softly, her eyes upon the ground]

Ah, that shall be when you please, dear friend.

HORACE

[almost choked with gratitude]

Oh!

[He kisses her hand.]

[HAWCASTLE and LADY CREECH enter from the garden, LADY CREECH talking excitedly.]

[ALMERIC enters through the gates.]

LADY CREECH

I tell you I couldn't hear a word they said, they mumbled their words so. But upon my soul, Hawcastle, if I couldn't hear, didn't I *see* enough?

HAWCASTLE

Upon my soul, I believe you did.

ALMERIC

Quite a family pow-wow you're havin'.

HAWCASTLE

Is there anything unusual in the village?

ALMERIC

Ra-ther! Carabiniere all over the shop—still huntin' that bandit feller.

LADY CREECH

Don't mumble your words!

ALMERIC

[shouting]

Lookin' for a bally bandit.

[She screams faintly.]

HAWCASTLE

Be quiet!

ALMERIC

He's still in this neighborhood, they think.

LADY CREECH

[to HAWCASTLE]

What did I tell you? Now, how long—

HAWCASTLE

You shall not repeat one word of what you saw. Almeric, find your betrothed and ask her to come here.

ALMERIC

Rumbo! I don't mind, pater!

[Exit into the hotel.]

HORACE

What's the row?

HAWCASTLE

My dear young man, I congratulate you that you and your sister need no longer submit to an odious dictation.

[Enter PIKE briskly from the hotel.]

PIKE

[as he enters, genially]

Looks to me like it was going to clear up cold.

[LADY CREECH haughtily stalks off into the garden.]

HAWCASTLE

[pleasantly]

Good-afternoon, Mr. Pike.

PIKE

[going to the motor]

Howdy!

[Begins touching different parts of the engine.]

[MADAME DE CHAMPIGNY and HORACE haughtily follow LADY CREECH.]

HAWCASTLE

[suavely, to PIKE]

Mr. Pike, it is an immense pity that there should have been any misunderstanding in the matter of your ward's betrothal.

PIKE

[looking up for a moment, mildly]

Oh, I wouldn't call it a misunderstanding.

HAWCASTLE

It would ill become a father to press upon the subject of his son's merits—

PIKE

[plaintively]

I don't want to talk about *him* with you—I don't want to hurt your feelings.

HAWCASTLE

Perhaps I might better put it on the ground of your ward's wishes— of certain advantages of position which it is her ambition to attain.

PIKE

[troubled]

I can't talk about it with anybody but her.

[Enter MARIANO from the hotel with a letter on a tray. Goes to PIKE.]

HAWCASTLE

There is another matter—

[PIKE stands examining envelope of the letter in profound thought.]

I fear I do not have your attention.

[MARIANO goes into the hotel.]

PIKE

[looking up]

Go ahead!

HAWCASTLE

There is *another* matter to which I may wish to call your attention.

PIKE

[genially]

Oh, I'll talk about anything *else* with you.

HAWCASTLE

[suavely]

This is a question distinctly different

[with a glance at the hotel, his voice growing somewhat threatening]

—distinctly!

[ETHEL enters from the hotel.]

ETHEL

[to HAWCASTLE, in a troubled voice]

You wished me to come here.

HAWCASTLE

[going to her and taking her hand]

My child, I wish you to have another chat with our strangely prejudiced friend on the subject so near to all our hearts. And I wish to tell you that I see light breaking through our clouds. Even if he prove obdurate, do not be downcast—all will be well.

[Turns and goes out into the garden, his voice coming back in benign, fatherly tones.]

All will be well!

[PIKE stands regarding ETHEL, who does not look up at him.]

PIKE

[gently]

I'm glad you've come, Miss Ethel. I've got something here I want to read to you.

ETHEL

[coldly]

I did not come to hear you read.

PIKE

When I got your letter at home I wrote to Jim Cooley, our vice-consul at London, to look up the records of these Hawcastle folks and write to me here about how they stand in their own community.

ETHEL

[astounded]

What!

94

PIKE

What's thought of them by the best citizens, and so on.

ETHEL

[enraged]

You had the audacity—*you*—to pry into the affairs of the Earl of Hawcastle!

PIKE

Why, I'd 'a' done that—I wouldn't 'a' stopped at anything—I'd' 'a' done that if it had been the Governor of Indiana himself!

ETHEL

You didn't consider it indelicate to write to strangers about my intimate affairs?

PIKE

[placatingly]

Why, Jim Cooley's home-folks! His office used to be right next to mine in Kokomo.

ETHEL

It's monstrous—and when *they* find what you've done—Oh, hadn't you shamed me enough without this?

PIKE

I expect this letter'll show who ought to be ashamed. Now just let's sit down here and try to work things out together.

ETHEL

[with a slight, bitter laugh]

"Work things out together!"

PIKE

I'm sorry—for *you*, I mean. But I don't see any other way to do it, except—together. Won't you?

95

[She moves slowly forward and sits at extreme left of the bench. He watches her, noticing how far she withdraws from him, bows his head humbly, with a sad smile, then sits, not quite at the extreme right of the bench, but near it.]

PIKE

I haven't opened the letter yet. I want you to read it first, but I ought to tell you there's probably things in it'll hurt your feelings, sort of, mebbe.

ETHEL

[icily]

How?

PIKE

Well, I haven't much of a doubt but Jim'll have some statements in it that'll show you I'm right about these people. If he's got the facts, I *know* he will.

ETHEL

How do you know it?

PIKE

Because I've had experience enough of life—

ETHEL

In Kokomo?

PIKE

Yes, ma'am! there's just as many kinds of people in Kokomo as there is in Pekin, and I didn't serve a term in the legislature without learning to pick underhand men at sight. Now that Earl, let alone his havin' a bad eye—his ways are altogether too much on the stripe of T. Cuthbert Bentley's to suit me.

[He opens the envelope slowly, continuing.]

T. Cuthbert was a Chicago gentleman with a fur-lined overcoat. He opened up a bank in our town, and when he caught the Canadian

96

express, three months later, all he left in Kokomo was the sign on the front door. That was *painted* on. And as for the son. But there—I don't know as I have a call to say more.

[Takes the letter from the envelope.]

Here's the letter; read it for yourself.

[Gives it to her, watching her as she reads.]

ETHEL

[reading]

"Dear Dan: The Earldom of Hawcastle is one of the oldest in the Kingdom, and the St. Aubyns have distinguished themselves in the forefront of English battles from Agincourt and Crecy to Sebastopol.

[She reads this in a ringing voice and glances at him.]

[PIKE looks puzzled and depressed.]

"The present holder of the title came into it unexpectedly through a series of accidental deaths. He was a younger son's younger son, and had spent some years in Russia in business—what, I do not know—under another name. I suppose he assumed it that the historic name of St. Aubyn might not be tarnished by association with trade. He has spent so much of his life out of England that it is difficult to find out a great deal about him. Nothing here in his English record is seriously against him; though everything he has is mortgaged over its value, the entail having been broken.

[ETHEL pauses and looks at PIKE, who, much disturbed, rises, and crosses the stage.]

"As to his son, the Honorable Almeric, there's no objection alleged against his character. That's all I've been able to learn."

[She finishes with an air of triumphant finality, and rises with a laugh.]

A terrible indictment! So that was what you counted on to convince me of my mistake?

PIKE

[distressed]

97

Yes—it *was!*

ETHEL

Do you assert there is *one* word in this seriously discreditable to the reputation of Lord Hawcastle or Mr. St. Aubyn?

PIKE

[humbly]

No.

ETHEL

And you remember, it is the testimony offered by your own friend

[scornfully]

—by your own detective!

PIKE

[ruefully]

Oh, if I wanted a detective I wouldn't get Jim Cooley—at least, not any *more!*

[His attitude is thoroughly crestfallen.]

ETHEL

[triumphantly, almost graciously]

I shall tell Lord Hawcastle that you will be ready to take up the matter of the settlement the moment his solicitor arrives.

PIKE

No, I wouldn't do that.

ETHEL

[in a challenging voice]

Why not?

PIKE

[doggedly]

Because I won't take up the matter of settlements with him or any one else.

ETHEL

[angrily]

Do you mean you cannot see what a humiliation your interference has brought upon you in this?

PIKE

No; I see that plain enough.

ETHEL

Have you, after this, any further objections to my alliance with Mr. St. Aubyn?

PIKE

It ain't an alliance with Mr. St. Aubyn that you're after.

ETHEL

Then what am I

[pauses and lays scornful emphasis on the next word]

after?

PIKE

[slowly]

You're after something there isn't anything to. If I'd let you buy what you want to with your money and your whole life, you'd find it as empty as the morning after Judgment Day.

[She turns from him, smiling and superior.]

You think because I'm a jay country lawyer I don't understand it and couldn't understand *you*! Why, we've got just the same thing at home. There was little Annie Hoffmeyer. Her pa was a carpenter and doing well. But Annie couldn't get into the Kokomo Ladies' Literary Club, and her name didn't show up in the society column four or five times every Saturday morning, so she got her pa to give her the money to marry Artie Seymour, the minister's son—and a *regular* minister's son he was! Almost broke Hoffmeyer's heart, but he let her have her way and went in debt and bought them a little house on North Main Street. That was two years ago. Annie's workin' at the depoe candy-stand now and Artie's workin' at the hotel bar—in front—drinking up what's left of old Hoffmeyer's—settlement!

ETHEL

[outraged]

And you say you understand—you who couple the name of a tippling yokel with that of a St. Aubyn—a gentleman of distinction.

PIKE

Distinction? I didn't know he was distinguished.

ETHEL

[in a ringing voice]

His ancestors have fought with glory on every field of battle from Crecy and Agincourt to the Crimea.

PIKE

But you won't *see* much of his *ancestors*.

ETHEL

He bears their name.

PIKE

[with authority and dignity]

Yes—and it's the *name* you want. Nobody could look at you and not know it wasn't *him*. It's the *name*! And I'd let you buy it if it would make you happy—if you didn't have to take the people with it.

[A deepening of color in the light shows that it has grown to be late afternoon, near sunset.]

ETHEL

[angrily]

The "people"?

PIKE

Yes; the whole gang. Can't you see how they're counting on it? It's in their faces, in their ways! This Earl—don't you see he's counting on living on you? Do you think the son would get that settlement? Why, a Terre Hut pickpocket could get it away from *him*—let alone his old man! What do *you* think would become of the "settlement"?

ETHEL

Part of it would go to the restoration of Hawcastle Hall and part to Glenwood Priory.

PIKE

Glenwood Priory?

ETHEL

That is part of the estate where Almeric and I will live until Lord Hawcastle's death.

PIKE

Then mighty little settlement would come around "Glenwood Priory"!

[Speaks the name as though grimly amused, and continues.]

And this old lady—this Mrs. Creech you been travelling with—

ETHEL

[sharply]

Lady Creech!

PIKE

All right! Don't you think *she's* counting on it? And this French lady that's with them; isn't she trying to land your brother? The whole crowd is on the track of John Simpson's money.

ETHEL

Silence! You have no right to traduce them. Do you place no value upon heredity, upon high birth?

PIKE

Why, I think so much of it that I know John Simpson's daughter doesn't need anybody else's to help her out.

[He comes toward her, looking at her with honest admiration.]

She's fine enough and I think she's sweet enough—and I know from the way she goes for me that she's *brave* enough—to stand on her own feet!

ETHEL

This is beside the point; I know exactly what I want in life—

[she has been somewhat moved by his last speech, is agitated, and a little breathless]

—and I could not change now if it were otherwise. I gave Almeric my promise, it was forever, and I shall keep it.

PIKE

But you can't; I'm not going to let you.

ETHEL

I throw your interference to the winds. I shall absolutely disregard it. I shall marry without your consent.

PIKE

[looking at her steadily]

Do you think *they'd* let you?

ETHEL

[in same tone]

I think *you'll* let me,

[laughing]

especially after this terrible letter.

PIKE

By-the-way, did you finish it?

[ETHEL looks at the letter, which she has continued to hold in her hand.]

ETHEL

I think so.

[Turns the page.]

No—it says "over."

[She turns the sheet—looks at it attentively for a moment—looks up, casts a quick glance of astonishment at PIKE.]

PIKE

Well, read it, please!

ETHEL

It appears to concern a matter quite personal to yourself.

[Embarrassed, assuming carelessness. Turns toward left as if to leave, replacing the letter in the envelope.]

PIKE

[advancing to her, smiling]

I don't think I've got any secrets.

ETHEL

[coldly]

Please remember, I have not read anything on the last page.

PIKE

Well, neither have I.

[Reaching his hand for the letter.]

ETHEL

[more embarrassed]

Oh!

[She drops the letter on the bench.]

[PIKE picks it up and walks slowly toward right, taking it from envelope. She stands looking after him with breathless amazement, far from hostile, yet half turned as if to go at once. PIKE, taking the letter out of the envelope, suddenly looks back at her. At this she is flustered and starts, but halts at sound of the "Fishermen's Song" in the distance. The sunset is deepening to golden red; the "Fishermen's Song" begins with mandolins and guitars, and then a number of voices are heard together.]

ETHEL

Listen: those are the fishermen coming home.

[PIKE stands in arrested attitude, not having looked at the letter. The song, beginning faintly, grows louder, then slowly dies away in the distance. The two stand listening in deepening twilight.]

PIKE

[as the voices cease to be heard]

It's mighty pretty, but it's kind of foreign and lonesome, too.

[With a sad half-chuckle.]

I'd rather hear something that sounded more like home.

[A growing tremulousness in his voice.]

I expect you've about forgot everything like that, haven't you?

104

ETHEL

[gently]

Yes.

PIKE

Seems funny, now; but out on the ocean, coming here, I kept kind of looking forward to hearing you sing. I knew how high your pa had you educated in music, and, like the old fool I was, I kept thinking you'd sing for me some evening—"Sweet Genevieve" mebbe. You know it—don't you?

ETHEL

[slowly]

"Sweet Genevieve?" I used to—but it's rather old-fashioned and common, isn't it?

PIKE

I expect so; I reckon mebbe that's the reason I like it so much.

[With an apologetic and pathetic laugh.]

Yes'm, it's my favorite. I couldn't—I couldn't get you to sing it for me before I go back home—could I?

ETHEL

I—I think not.

[She looks at him thoughtfully, then goes slowly into the hotel.]

[PIKE sighs, and begins to read the last page of the letter.]

PIKE

[reading]

"I am sorry old man Simpson's daughter thinks of buying a title. Somehow I have a notion that that may hit you, Dan.

[Poignant dismay and awe are expressed in his voice as he continues.]

105

"I haven't forgotten how you always kept that picture of her on your desk. The old man thought so much of you I had an idea he hoped she'd come back some day and marry a man from home."

I don't wonder she said she hadn't read it!

[His face begins to light with radiant amazement.]

But she *had*—and she didn't go away—that is, not *right* away!

[LORD HAWCASTLE and HORACE enter from the hotel.]

HORACE

[speaking as they enter]

But, Lord Hawcastle, Ethel says Mr. Pike positively refuses.

HAWCASTLE

Leave him to me. Within ten minutes he will be as meek as a nun.

[HORACE goes into the hotel.]

My dear Pike, there is a certain question—

PIKE

[in his mildest tone]

I don't want to seem rough with you, but I meant what I said.

HAWCASTLE

Imagining I did not mean *that* question—

PIKE

Then it's all right.

HAWCASTLE

Late this afternoon I developed a great anxiety concerning the penalty prescribed by Italian law for those unfortunate and impulsive individuals who connive at the escape or concealment—

[he speaks with significant emphasis and a glance at the hotel, where lights begin to appear in the windows]

—of certain other unfortunates who may be, to speak vulgarly, wanted—by the police.

PIKE

[coolly]

You're anxious about that, are you?

HAWCASTLE

So deeply that I ascertained the penalty for it. You may confirm my information by appealing to the nearest carabiniere—strange to say, many of them are very near. The minimum penalty for one whose kind heart has thus betrayed him—

[he turns up sharply toward the lighted windows of hotel, then sharply again to PIKE, his voice lifting]

—is two years' imprisonment, and Italian prisons, I am credibly informed, are quite ferociously unpleasant.

PIKE

[gently]

Well, being in jail *any* place ain't much like an Elks' carnival.

HAWCASTLE

There would be no escape, even for a citizen of your admirable country, if his complicity were established, especially if he happened to be—as it were—caught in the act!

PIKE

[grimly]

Talk plain; talk plain.

HAWCASTLE

My dear young friend, imagine that a badly wanted man appears upon the pergola here and makes an appeal of I know not what nature to one of your fellow-countrymen, who—for the purposes of argument—is at work upon this car. Say that the too-amiable American conceals the fugitive under the automobile, and

107

afterward, with the connivance of a friend, deceives the officers of the law and shelters the criminal, say in a room of that lower suite yonder.

[His voice shows growing excitement as a man's shadow appears on the shade of the window nearest the door.]

Imagine, for instance, that the shadow which at this moment appears on the curtain were that of the wanted man—*then*, would you not agree that a moderate and reasonable request of your fellow-countryman might be acceded to?

PIKE

[swallowing painfully]

What would be the nature of that request?

HAWCASTLE

It would concern a certain alliance; *might* concern a certain settlement.

PIKE

If the request were refused, what would the consequences be?

HAWCASTLE

Two years, at least, for the American, and the friend who had been his accessory. Altogether I should consider it a disastrous situation.

PIKE

[thoughtfully]

Yes; looks like it.

HAWCASTLE

[with sharp significance]

If this fellow-countryman of yours were assured that the law would be made to take its course if a favorable answer were not received— say, by ten o'clock to-night—what, in your opinion, would his answer be?

PIKE

[plaintively]

Well, it would all depend upon which of my countrymen you caught. If it depended on the one I know best, he'd tell you he'd see you in *hell* first!

[The two remain staring fixedly at each other as the curtain slowly descends.]

END OF THE SECOND ACT

THE THIRD ACT

SCENE: A handsome private salon in the hotel the same evening. There are cabinets against the walls, buhl tables, luxurious tapestried chairs, etc. At back, double doors, wide open, disclose a brilliantly lit conservatory and hall with palms and oleanders in bloom. On the left a heavily curtained window looks out upon the garden; on the right is a closed door. Unseen, an orchestra is playing an aria from "Pagliacci."

The rise of the curtain discloses PIKE sitting in a dejected attitude in an arm-chair. He wears a black tie, collar and linen as before, black trousers, a white waistcoat, cut rather low, and a black frock-coat—"Western statesman" style—not fashionably cut, but well-fitting and graceful.

MARIANO passes through the conservatory at back bearing a coffee-tray. LADY CREECH, in an evening gown of black velvet and lace, follows with stately tread. HORACE, in evening clothes, follows, with MADAME DE CHAMPIGNY on his arm; she is in a handsome, very Parisian, décolleté dress. They are deep in tender conversation.

ETHEL follows, on the arm of ALMERIC. She wears a pretty evening gown, ALMERIC in evening clothes; her head is bent, her eyes cast down.

A valet de chambre enters the salon from the hall. He touches an electric button on wall near door. RIBIERE comes quickly and noiselessly from the room to the right. They stand bowing as VASILI enters through the conservatory. Valet immediately closes the doors. VASILI wears an overcoat trimmed with sables, a silk hat, evening clothes, and white gloves; order ribbon in his button-hole.

PIKE

[as VASILI enters]

I'm mighty glad you've come—I've been waiting.

110

VASILI

[to RIBIERE, and speaking in undertone]

You have telegraphed for the information?

RIBIERE

Yes, sir.

[Valet, with coat, hat, etc., goes out, followed by RIBIERE.]

VASILI

I have dined with an old tutor of mine. Once every year I come here to do that.

[Valet returns with vodka and cigarettes, which he places on a table, immediately withdrawing.]

VASILI

[with a keen glance at PIKE]

And you; I suppose you dined with the charming young lady, your ward, and her brother, as you expected?

PIKE

[turning away sadly]

Oh no, they've got friends of their own here.

VASILI

So I have observed.

[Sips vodka.]

PIKE

Oh, I don't mind their not asking me.

[With an assumption of cheerfulness.]

Fact is, these friends of hers are trying to get me to do something I can't do—

111

VASILI

You need not tell me that, my friend. I have both eyes and ears; I understand.

PIKE

[troubled, coming near him]

I wish you understood the rest, because it ain't easy for me to tell you. Doc, I'm afraid I've got you into a pretty bad hole.

VASILI

[smiling]

Ah, that I fear I do not understand.

PIKE

[remorsefully]

I'm afraid I have. You and Ivanoff and me—all three of us. This Hawcastle knows, and he knows it as well as I know you're sittin' in that chair, that we've got that poor fellow in yonder.

[Pointing to the door on the right.]

VASILI

Surely you can trust Lord Hawcastle not to mention it. He must know that the consequences for you, as well as for me, would be, to say the least, disastrous. Surely you made that clear to him.

PIKE

[grimly]

No; he made it clear to me. Two years in jail is the minimum, and if I don't make up my mind by ten o'clock

[VASILI looks at his watch]

to do what he wants me to do—

VASILI

What does he want you to do?

PIKE

The young lady's father trusted me to look after her, and if I won't promise to let her pay seven hundred and fifty thousand dollars for that—well, you've seen it around here, haven't you—

VASILI

I have observed it—that is, if you refer to the son of Lord Hawcastle.

PIKE

Well, if I don't consent to do that, I reckon Ivanoff has to go back to Siberia and you and I to jail.

VASILI

He threatens that?

PIKE

He'll *do* that!

VASILI

[looking at him sharply]

What do *you* mean to do?

PIKE

There wouldn't be any trouble about it if it was only me. That would make it easy. They could land me for two years

[swallowing painfully]

or twenty. What makes it so hard is that I can't do what they want, even to let you and Ivanoff out. It ain't my money. All I can do is to ask you to forgive me, and warn you to get away before they come down on me. This feller's *got* me, Doc. Don't you see how it stands? Ivanoff can't get away—

VASILI

No; I think he can't.

PIKE

They've got this militia all around the place.

VASILI

I passed through the cordon of carabiniere as I came in.

PIKE

[urgently]

But you could get away, Doc. Up to ten o'clock you can come and go as you choose.

VASILI

[rising]

So can you. You have not thought of that?

PIKE

No; and I won't think of it. But as for you—

VASILI

As for me

[rings bell near door]

—I shall go!

PIKE

That's part of the load off my mind. I can't bear to think of the rest of it. I haven't known how to tell that poor fellow in there.

[Valet enters.]

VASILI

[to valet, indicating the door on the right]

Appellez le Monsieur la.

[Valet goes to the door, opens it, bowing slightly to IVANOFF, who appears. Valet withdraws.]

[IVANOFF is very pale and haggard looking, but his clothes have been mended and neatly brushed. He comes in slowly and quietly.]

VASILI

[in the tone of a superior]

You may come in, Ivanoff. Some unexpected difficulties have arisen. Your presence here has been discovered by persons who wish evil to this gentleman who has protected you. He can do nothing further to save you unless he betrays a trust which has been left to him.

[IVANOFF swallows painfully, and looks pitifully from VASILI to PIKE.]

PIKE

[coming down to IVANOFF, standing before him humbly]

It's the truth, old man. I can't do it.

[IVANOFF'S head falls forward on his chest.]

IVANOFF

[in a low voice]

I thank you for what you have tried to do for me.

[Gives PIKE his hand. PIKE turns away.]

VASILI

You have until ten o'clock.

[Valet appears in the doorway.]

Mon chapeau et pardessus.

[Exit valet.]

In the meantime my friend believes Naples a safe place for me.

[Valet returns with his coat, hat, and gloves.]

And so, auf weidersehn.

[Dismisses the valet with a gesture.]

PIKE

[going to him and shaking hands heartily]

Good-bye, Doc, and God bless you!

VASILI

To our next meeting.

[Exit briskly through the upper doors. As they close behind him, IVANOFF'S manner changes. He goes rapidly to a table, picks up the cigarettes, which are in a large silver open box, and touches the bottle of vodka significantly.]

IVANOFF

I thought so—Russian!

PIKE

What!

IVANOFF

That man, your friend, who calls himself Gröllerhagen, is not a German—he is a Russian—not only that, he is a Russian noble. I see it in a hundred ways that you cannot.

PIKE

Whatever he is, he helped us this afternoon. I'd trust him to the bone.

IVANOFF

I have felt it inevitable that I should go back to Siberia. A thousand times have I felt it since I entered these rooms.

[He goes down toward the window.]

PIKE

I know you feel mighty bad, but perhaps—perhaps—

116

IVANOFF

There is no perhaps for me. There was never any perhaps after I met Hélène.

PIKE

[scratching his head]

Hélène!

IVANOFF

Hélène was my wife, she who sent me to Siberia, she and my dear, accursed English friend.

PIKE

[thoughtfully]

What was his name?

IVANOFF

His name—it was Glenwood. I shall not forget that name soon.

PIKE

What was he doing in Russia?

IVANOFF

I have told you he had contracts with the Ministry of Finance—he supplied hydraulic machinery to the government. Does the name Glenwood mean anything to you? Have you heard it?

PIKE

[profoundly thoughtful, pauses, looking at IVANOFF sharply]

No.

[Then to himself.]

And there must be a million Hélènes in France.

IVANOFF

I prayed God to let me meet them before I was taken. But I talk too

117

much of myself. I wish to know—you—you will be safe. They can do nothing to you, can they?

PIKE

[with assumed cheerfulness]

Oh, I'm all right—don't worry about me.

[Loud knock at the upper doors.]

IVANOFF

[despairingly]

It is the carabiniere.

PIKE

Steady.

[Looks at watch.]

Not yet. Go back. We won't throw our hands into the discard until we're called. We'll keep on raising.

[Exit IVANOFF through door on the right, closing it after him.]

[PIKE scratches his head and slowly says: "Hélène." Then calls: "Come in!"]

[MARIANO opens the upper doors from without and bows.]

MARIANO

Miladi Creesh—she ask you would speak with her a few minutes?

PIKE

All right! Where is she?

MARIANO

Here, sir.

PIKE

Come right in, ma'am!

[LADY CREECH enters.]

LADY CREECH

[frigidly]

I need scarcely inform you that this interview is not of my seeking.

[She sits stiffly.]

On the contrary, it is intensely disagreeable to me. My brother-in-law feels that some one well acquainted with Miss Granger-Simpson's ambitions and her inner nature should put the case finally to you before we proceed to extremities.

PIKE

Yes, ma'am!

LADY CREECH

[crossly]

Don't mumble your words if you expect me to listen to you.

PIKE

[cordially]

Go on, ma'am!

LADY CREECH

My brother-in-law has made us aware of the state of affairs, and we are quite in sympathy with my brother-in-law's attitude as to what should be done to you.

PIKE

[in a tone of genial inquiry]

Yes, ma'am; and what do you think ought to be done to me?

LADY CREECH

If, in the kindness of our hearts, we condone your offence, we insist upon your accession to our reasonable demands.

119

PIKE

[sardonically]

By ten o'clock!

LADY CREECH

Quite so.

PIKE

You say he told all of you? Has he told Miss Ethel?

LADY CREECH

It hasn't been thought proper. Young girls should be shielded from everything disagreeable.

PIKE

Yes, ma'am; that's the idea that got me into this trouble.

LADY CREECH

I say, this young lady, who seems to be technically your ward, is considered, by all of us who understand her, infinitely more *my* ward.

PIKE

Yes, ma'am! Go on.

LADY CREECH

[loftily]

She came to me something more than a year ago—

PIKE

[simply]

Did you advertise?

LADY CREECH

[stung]

I suppose it is your intention to be offensive.

PIKE

[protesting]

No, ma'am; I didn't mean anything. But, you see, I've handled all her accounts, and her payments to you—

LADY CREECH

[crushingly]

We will omit tradesman-like references! What Lord Hawcastle wished me to impress on you is not only that you will ruin yourself, but put a blight upon the life of the young lady whom you are pleased to consider your ward. We make this suggestion because we conceive that you have a preposterous sentimental interest yourself in Miss Granger-Simpson.

PIKE

[taken aback]

Me?

LADY CREECH

Upon what other ground are we to explain your conduct?

PIKE

You mean that I'd only stand between her and you for my own sake?

LADY CREECH

We can comprehend no other grounds.

PIKE

[solemnly]

I don't believe you can! But you *can* comprehend that I wouldn't have any hope, can't you?

LADY CREECH

One never knows what these weird Americans hope. Hawcastle

121

assures me you have some such idea, but my charge has studied under my instruction—deportment, manners, and ideals—which has lifted her above the mere American circumstance of her birth. She has ambitions. If you stand in the way of them she will wither, she will die like a caged bird. All that was sordid about her parentage she has cast off. We have thought that we might make something out of her.

PIKE

[in a clear voice, looking at her mildly]

Make *something* out of her—yes, *ma'am!*

LADY CREECH

[quickly]

Make something *better* of her. We offer her this alliance with a family which for seven hundred years—

PIKE

Yes, ma'am—Crecy and Agincourt—I know.

LADY CREECH

With a family never sullied by those low ideals of barter and exchange which are the governing impulses of your countrymen.

PIKE

Seven hundred years—

[fumbling in coat-pocket]

—why, look here, Mrs. Creech!

[At this LADY CREECH half rises from her chair with a profound shudder, sinks back again; PIKE continues.]

I've got a letter right here

[takes letter from pocket]

that tells me your brother-in-law was in business—and I respect him for it—only a few years ago.

122

LADY CREECH

[angrily]

A letter from whom?

PIKE

Jim Cooley, our vice-consul in London. Jim ain't the wisest man in the world, but he seems to have this all right, and *he* says Mr. Hawcastle—

LADY CREECH

[exploding]

Mr. Hawcastle!

PIKE

[placatingly]

Well, I can call a person Colonel or Cap or Doc or anything of that kind, but I just plain don't know how to use the kind of words you have over here for those things. They don't seem to fit my mouth, somehow. Just let me run on my own way. I don't mean to hurt your feelings. Anyway, Jim says your brother-in-law was in business in Russia.

[Up to this point he has gone on rapidly, but after the word "Russia" he pauses abruptly as if startled by a sudden thought and slowly repeats.]

"In business in Russia!"

[He rises.]

LADY CREECH

This is beside the point entirely!

PIKE

It *is* the point! Now, between us, ain't Jim right? Ain't it the truth?

LADY CREECH

[angry and agitated]

123

Since some of your vulgar American officials have been spying about—

PIKE

[with controlled excitement]

Your brother-in-law was in business in Russia; so far, so good.

[Leans upon back of chair watching her, eager, but smiling cordially.]

I don't say he was peddling shoe-strings on the corner or selling weinerwursts—

[LADY CREECH gives a slight scream of indignation.]

PIKE

[continuing]

Probably something more hifalutin' and dignified than that. He was probably agent for a wooden butter-dish factory.

LADY CREECH

[enraged]

He had contracts with the Russian government itself!

PIKE

(staggering back, recovers himself immediately, and, speaking sharply, but in a voice of great agitation). *Not* for mining—*not* for hydraulic machines!

LADY CREECH

And even so he protected the historic name of St. Aubyn.

PIKE

By God, I believe you!

LADY CREECH

Don't mumble your words!

PIKE

Had he ever lived at Glenwood Priory?

LADY CREECH

[indignantly]

Is your mind wandering? The priory belonged to Hawcastle's mother. Can you state its connection with the subject?

PIKE

That's how he protected the historic name of St. Aubyn! That's the name he took—Glenwood!

LADY CREECH

What of that?

PIKE

[awe-struck]

God moves in a mysterious way his wonders to perform!

LADY CREECH

Oblige me by omitting blasphemous allusions in my presence. What answer are you prepared to make to Lord Hawcastle?

PIKE

[in a ringing voice]

Tell your brother-in-law that he can have my answer in ten minutes—and he can come to me *here* for it! I'll give it in the presence of the young lady and her brother.

LADY CREECH

[turning to go]

Her brother—certainly! He is in perfect sympathy with our attitude. As for Miss Granger-Simpson's knowing anything of this most disagreeable affair—no!

PIKE

I beg your pardon.

LADY CREECH

I shall not permit her to come near here. As her chaperone I refuse. We all refuse!

PIKE

All right; refuse away.

LADY CREECH

I shall tell Lord Hawcastle—

PIKE

Ten minutes from now and in this room.

LADY CREECH

But Miss Granger-Simpson under no condition whatever.

[Sweeps out haughtily.]

[PIKE closes the doors behind her, touches an electric button over the mantel, then sits at desk and writes hurriedly. Knock at upper doors.]

PIKE

Come in!

[Enter MARIANO.]

PIKE

Mariano, I want you to take this note to Miss Simpson.

[Quickly enclosing note in envelope and addressing it.]

MARIANO

To Mees Granger-Seempson?

PIKE

Do you know where she is?

MARIANO

She walks on the terrace alone.

PIKE

Give it to her yourself—to no one else—

[emphatically]

—and do it now.

[Gives him the note.]

MARIANO

At once, sir!

[Going.]

PIKE

Hurry!

[Almost pushes him out of the upper doors and closes them. He goes quickly to the door on the right, opens it, and calls.]

Ivanoff!

[IVANOFF opens the door and comes out apprehensively.]

IVANOFF

[as he enters]

Have they come?

PIKE

Not yet! Ivanoff, you prayed to see your wife and your friend Glenwood before you went back to Siberia.

IVANOFF

[falling back with a cry]

Ah!

PIKE

If that prayer is answered through me, will you promise to remember that it's my fight?

IVANOFF

Ah! it is impossible—you wish to play with me!

PIKE

Do I look playful?

[A bugle sounds sharply outside the window.]

IVANOFF

[wildly]

The carabiniere—for me.

[The two rush together to the window.]

PIKE

[thrusting IVANOFF behind him]

Don't show yourself!

IVANOFF

[looking out of the window over PIKE'S shoulder]

Look! Near the lamp yonder—there by the doors—the carabiniere.

PIKE

They've been there since this afternoon.

[Shading his eyes from the light of the room with one hand.]

Look there—who on earth—who's that they've got with them?—Why, good Lord! it's Doc!

[Astounded.]

IVANOFF

It is Herr von Gröllerhagen! Did I not tell you he was a Russian? He has betrayed me himself. He was not satisfied that others should.

[Bitterly.]

I knew I was in the wolf's throat here!

PIKE

Don't you believe it! They've arrested poor old Doc. They got him as he went out.

IVANOFF

[pointing]

No; they speak respectfully to him. They bow to him—

PIKE

[grimly]

They'll be bowing to us in a minute. That's probably the way these colonels run you in.

[Sharp knock on upper doors.]

PIKE

[urging him toward the door on the right]

You wait till I call you, and remember it's my fight.

IVANOFF

[turning, half hysterically]

You *promise* before I am taken that I shall see—

[MARIANO enters at upper doors.]

PIKE

[domineeringly, as he sees MARIANO]

And don't you forget what I've been telling you—you get the sand out of that gear-box first thing tomorrow morning, or I'll see that you draw your last pay Saturday night.

[IVANOFF bows meekly and exit to right, closing door after him.]

MARIANO

Miss Granger-Seempson!

[Exit.]

PIKE

All right, Mariano!

[ETHEL enters haughtily.]

I'm much obliged to you for taking my note the right way. I've got some pretty good reasons for not leaving this room.

[She is icy in manner, but her hands fidget with the note he has sent her, crumpling it up.]

ETHEL

[sitting]

Your note seemed so extraordinarily urgent—

PIKE

It had to be. Some folks who want to see me are coming here, and I want you to see them—here. They'd stopped you from coming if they could.

ETHEL

[holding herself very straight in her chair]

There was no effort to prevent me.

PIKE

No; I didn't give 'em time.

ETHEL

May I ask to whom you refer?

130

PIKE

The whole kit and boodle of 'em!

ETHEL

[not relaxing her coldness]

You are inelegant, Mr. Pike.

PIKE

I haven't time to be elegant, even if I knew how.

ETHEL

Do you mean that my chaperone would disapprove?

PIKE

I shouldn't be surprised. I reckon the whole fine flower of Europe would disapprove. "Disapprove?"—they'd *sand-bag* you to keep you away!

ETHEL

[rising quickly]

Oh, then I can't stay.

PIKE

[going between her and the upper doors, speaks with ring of domination]

Yes you can, and you will, and you've got to!

ETHEL

[angrily]

"Got to!" I shall not!

PIKE

I'm your guardian, and you'll do as I say. You'll obey me this once if you never do again.

[She looks at him defiantly; he faces her with determination, and continues without pause.]

You'll stay here while I talk to these people, and you'll stay in spite of anything they say or do to make you go.

[Slight pause; she yields and walks back to her chair. PIKE continues.]

God knows I hate to talk rough to you. I wouldn't hurt your feelings for the world, but it's come to a point where I've got to use the authority I have over you.

ETHEL

[with a renewal of her defiance]

Authority? Do you think—

PIKE

You'll stay here for the next twenty minutes if I have to make Crecy and Agincourt look like a Peace Conference!

[She looks at him aghast, sinks into chair by table; he continues after a very slight pause.]

You and your brother have soaked up a society-column notion of life over here; you're like old Pete Delaney of Terry Hut—he got so he'd drink cold tea if there was a whiskey label on the bottle. They've fuddled you with labels. It's my business to see that you know what kind of people you're dealin' with.

ETHEL

[almost in tears]

You're bullying me! I don't see why you talk so brutally to me.

PIKE

[sadly and earnestly]

Do you think I'd do it for anything but you?

ETHEL

[angrily]

132

You are odious! Insufferable!

PIKE

[humbly]

Don't you think I know you despise me?

ETHEL

I do not despise you; if I had stayed at home, and grown up there, I should probably have been a provincial young woman playing "Sweet Genevieve" for you to-night. But my life has not been that, and you have humiliated me from the moment of your arrival here. You have made me ashamed both of you and of myself. And now you have some preposterous plan which will shame me again, humiliate both of us once more, before my friends, these gentlefolk.

[A loud noise without. LADY CREECH'S voice is heard shouting.]

PIKE

[dryly]

I think the gentlefolk are here.

[The upper doors up centre are thrown open; LADY CREECH hurriedly enters, with MADAME DE CHAMPIGNY and HORACE, followed by ALMERIC.]

LADY CREECH

My dear child, what are you doing in this dreadful place with this dreadful person?

MADAME DE CHAMPIGNY

My dear, les convenances!

HORACE

Ethel, I'm extremely surprised; come away at once!

ALMERIC

Oh, I say, you know, really, Miss Ethel! You can't stay here, you know, *can* you?

PIKE

I'm her guardian; she's here by my authority, she'll stay by my authority.

[LORD HAWCASTLE appears in the open doors and bows sardonically to PIKE.]

HAWCASTLE

[suavely]

Ah, good-evening, Mr. Pike!

HORACE

Lord Hawcastle, will you insist upon Ethel's leaving? It's quite on the cards we shall have a disagreeable scene here.

HAWCASTLE

[smiling]

I see no occasion for it; we're here simply for Mr. Pike's answer. He knows where we stand and we know where he stands.

PIKE

[with a grim smile]

I reckon you're right so far.

HAWCASTLE

[continuing]

And his answer will be yes.

PIKE

[with quiet emphasis]

But you're wrong there!

HAWCASTLE

[to HORACE, with sudden seriousness]

Perhaps you are right, Mr. Granger-Simpson. Painful things may be done. Better the young lady were spared them. Take your sister away.

[He motions HORACE toward the door.]

ALMERIC

For God's sake do—it may be quite rowdy.

LADY CREECH

[to ETHEL at the same time]

My dear, you positively must!

HORACE

Ethel, I command you!

[ETHEL, troubled, half rises as if to go]

PIKE

[imperiously, to ETHEL]

You stay right where you are!

ALMERIC

[angrily]

Oh, I say!

LADY CREECH

Oh, the lynching ruffian!

HORACE

Ethel, do you mean to let this fellow dictate to you?

ETHEL

[breathlessly and loudly, as if resistance were hopeless]

But—he says I *must*!

[She sinks back into her chair.]

PIKE

[to HAWCASTLE]

You're here for an answer, you say?

HAWCASTLE

[on the defensive]

Yes!

PIKE

An answer to what?

HAWCASTLE

[painfully resuming his suavity]

An answer to our request that you accede to the wishes of that young lady.

PIKE

And if I don't, what are you going to do?

HORACE

Ethel, you *must* go!

MADAME DE CHAMPIGNY

This man is an Apache!

LADY CREECH

[simultaneously]

Barbarian!

PIKE

[to HAWCASTLE]

I'll leave it to you to tell her.

136

HAWCASTLE

A gentleman would spare her that.

PIKE

I won't! Speak out! Why do you come here sure of the answer you want?

HAWCASTLE

[intensely annoyed]

Tut, tut!

LADY CREECH

Don't mumble your words!

PIKE

I'll make it even plainer than you like.

HORACE

I protest against this!

ALMERIC

Throw the rotter out of the window!

PIKE

[particularly addressing ETHEL]

This afternoon I tried to help a poor devil—a broken-down Russian running away from Siberia, where he'd been for nine years.

[She rises; her eyes eagerly meet his.]

A poor weak thing, hounded like you've seen a rat in the gutter by dogs and bootblacks. Some of your friends here saw us bring him into this apartment; they know we've got him here now. If I don't agree to hand over you and seven hundred and fifty thousand dollars of the money John Simpson made, it means that the man I have tried to help goes back to rot in Siberia and I go to an Italian jail for two years, or as much longer as they can make it.

137

HAWCASTLE

[violently]

Nonsense!

ETHEL

[stepping toward PIKE, indignantly]

I knew that you had only a further humiliation in store for me—

HAWCASTLE

[following her and trying to interrupt]

But my dear—

ETHEL

[with dignity]

No—you need make no denial for yourselves.

[To PIKE, haughtily.]

Do you think I would believe that an English noble would stoop—

PIKE

[with passionate indignation]

Stoop! Why, ten years ago in St. Petersburg there was a poor revolutionist who, in his crazy patriotism, took government money for the cause he believed in. He made the mistake of keeping that money in his house, when this man

[pointing at HAWCASTLE]

knew it was there. He also made the mistake of having a wife that this man coveted and stole—as he coveted and stole the money. Oh, he made a good job of it! Don't think that to-night is the first time he has given information to the police. He did it then, and the husband went to Siberia—

HAWCASTLE

[staggered and enraged]

A dastardly slander!

PIKE

[in a ringing voice]

—and he'll do it again to-night. I go to an Italian jail

[he suddenly swings his outstretched hand to point to MADAME DE CHAMPIGNY, continuing without pause]

and, by the living God, that same poor devil of a husband goes back to Siberia!

[MADAME DE CHAMPIGNY, with an ejaculation of horror and fright, staggers back.]

HAWCASTLE

[in extreme agitation]

It's a ghastly lie!

PIKE

You came for your answer. Here it is.

[Calls sharply.]

Ivanoff!

[IVANOFF appears in the doorway on the right. He advances, lifts both clinched fists above MADAME DE CHAMPIGNY'S head.]

[MADAME DE CHAMPIGNY, with a shuddering cry, falls on her knees in an attitude of fright and abasement.]

MADAME DE CHAMPIGNY

Ivan!—oh, Mother of God!—Ivan! Don't kill me—

[IVANOFF shudders with weakness, trembles violently, collapses into chair, she still at his feet. IVANOFF sobbing.]

HORACE

[starting toward her in extreme agitation]

139

Hélène!

PIKE

[sternly to HORACE]

You keep back, she's his wife.

[Pointing to HAWCASTLE.]

And there stands his best friend!

HAWCASTLE

It's a lie! I never saw the man before in my life.

PIKE

[grimly, with a gesture toward MADAME DE CHAMPIGNY]

The lady seems to recognize him.

HAWCASTLE

Almeric, go for the police. Call them quickly!

[His voice loud and hoarse.]

MADAME DE CHAMPIGNY

[springs to her feet, protesting]

No—no—I can't!

PIKE

[with his hand on IVANOFF'S shoulder]

Call them in—we're ready.

[To ETHEL.]

But I want *you* always to remember that I considered it cheap at the price.

[ETHEL, in an agony of shame, turns from him. At same time MADAME DE CHAMPIGNY, never taking her eyes from

IVANOFF'S face, and showing great fear, moves back near HAWCASTLE.]

ALMERIC

[opening the upper doors and calling]

Tell that officer to bring his men in here!

[VASILI enters briskly from the hall.]

[RIBIERE enters immediately after from the same direction.]

VASILI

[in a loud, clear voice]

There will be no arrests to-night, my friends.

HAWCASTLE

[violently, to ALMERIC]

Do as I say! This man

[meaning VASILI]

goes, too.

VASILI

[curtly]

The officer is not there, the carabiniere have been withdrawn.

[To PIKE, gravely and rapidly.]

For your sake I have relinquished my incognito.

[To HAWCASTLE.]

The man Ivanoff is in my custody.

HAWCASTLE

[violently]

By whose authority? Do you know that you are speaking to the Earl of Hawcastle?

RIBIERE

[in a ringing voice, advancing a step]

More respectful, sir! You are addressing his Highness, the Grand-Duke Vasili of Russia.

[HAWCASTLE falls back, stricken.]

PIKE

[thunderstruck]

Respectful! Think of what *I've* been calling him!

VASILI

My friend, it has been refreshing.

[To RIBIERE]

Ribiere, I shall take Ivanoff's statement in writing. Bring him with you.

[VASILI turns on his heel, curtly, and passes rapidly out through the door on the right.]

[RIBIERE touches IVANOFF on shoulder, indicating that he must follow VASILI.]

[IVANOFF starts with RIBIERE; MADAME DE CHAMPIGNY shrinks back with a low exclamation of fear.]

IVANOFF

[hoarsely to her]

I would not touch you—not even to strangle you!

[With outstretched hand, pointing to HAWCASTLE.]

But God will let me pay my debt to the Earl of Hawcastle!

[Goes rapidly out with RIBIERE.]

HAWCASTLE

[choked with rage, advancing on PIKE]

Why, you—

PIKE

[genially]

Oh! I hated to hand you this, my lord. I didn't come over here to make the fine flower of Europe any more trouble than they've got. But I had to *show* John Simpson's daughter.

[Movement from HORACE and ETHEL.]

And I reckon now she isn't wanting any alliance with the remnants of Crecy and Agincourt.

ETHEL

[tremulously, coming close to PIKE]

But I have no choice—I gave Almeric my promise when I thought it an honor to bear his name. Now that you have shown me it is a *shame* to bear it, the promise is only more sacred. The shame is not *his* fault. You—you—want me to be—honorable—don't you?

PIKE

[after a long stare at her, speaks in a feeble voice, very slowly]

Your father—and mother—*both*—came—from Missouri, didn't they?

END OF THE THIRD ACT

THE FOURTH ACT

SCENE: The same as in Act I. The morning of the next day. Upon the steps leading to the hotel doors is a pile of bags, hat-boxes, and rugs.

As the curtain rises HAWCASTLE, in a travelling suit and cap, is directing a porter who is adjusting a strap on a travelling bag. ALMERIC enters from the hotel, smoking a cigarette.

ALMERIC

Ah, Governor; see you're moving!

HAWCASTLE

I may.

[His manner is nervous, apprehensive, and wary. Porter touches his cap and goes into hotel.]

It depends.

ALMERIC

Depends? Madame de Champigny took the morning boat to Naples, and your trunks are gone. Shouldn't say that looked much like dependin'.

HAWCASTLE

[nervously]

It does, though, with that devilish convict—

ALMERIC

Oh, but I say, Governor, you're not in a funk about him! You could bowl him over with a finger.

HAWCASTLE

[glancing over his shoulder]

144

Not if he had what he didn't have last night, or I shouldn't be here to-day.

ALMERIC

You don't think the beggar'd be taking a shot at you?

HAWCASTLE

[fastening clasp of hat-box]

I don't know what the crazy fool mightn't do.

ALMERIC

But, you know, he's really quite as much in custody as you could wish. That Vasilivitch chap has got him fast enough.

[LADY CREECH enters from the hotel.]

HAWCASTLE

[sharply]

The Grand-Duke Vasili has the reputation of being a romantic fool. I don't know what moment he may decide to let Ivanoff loose.

LADY CREECH

[with triumphant indignation]

Then I have the advantage over you, Hawcastle. He's just done it.

HAWCASTLE

[startled]

What?

LADY CREECH

[continuing]

Got him a pardon from Russia by telegraph.

HAWCASTLE

You don't mean that!

145

LADY CREECH

Ethel has just told me.

HAWCASTLE

My God!

[He springs forward and touches a bell on wall.]

LADY CREECH

An outrage! Our plans all so horribly upset—

HAWCASTLE

[turning and coming down steps]

No, they're not.

[MARIANO appears in the doorway.]

HAWCASTLE

Mariano, I'm off for Naples. Sharp's the word!

MARIANO

It is too late for the boat, Milor'. You must drive to Castellamare for the train.

HAWCASTLE

There's a carriage waiting for me at the gate yonder. Get these things into it quick—quick!

[MARIANO beckons porters from the hotel. Porters enter sharply and carry bags, etc., off.]

[Meanwhile, HAWCASTLE, without pause, continues rapidly and in an excited voice to ALMERIC and LADY CREECH.]

You must see it through; you mustn't let the thing fail; what's more, you've got to hurry it, just as if I were here. This girl gave her word last night that she'd stick.

146

LADY CREECH

But she's behaving very peculiarly this morning. Outrageously would be nearer it.

HAWCASTLE

How?

LADY CREECH

Shedding tears over this Ivanoff's story. What's more, she has sent that dreadful Pike person to him with assistance.

HAWCASTLE

What sort of assistance?

LADY CREECH

Money. I don't know how much, but I'm sure it was a lot.

ALMERIC

[with a sudden inspiration]

By Jove! Buying the beggar off, perhaps, to keep him from making a scandal for us.

HAWCASTLE

[excitedly]

That's what she's trying to do!

LADY CREECH

Then why do you go?

HAWCASTLE

Because I'm not sure she can.

[Going to steps.]

Wire me at the Bertolini, Naples.

[Turning at stoop.]

147

This shows she means to stick.

LADY CREECH

For the sake of her promise.

HAWCASTLE

[emphatically]

Yes, and for the sake of the name.

[He runs out rapidly.]

[PIKE enters from the grove, smoking.]

PIKE

[thoughtfully]

Your pa seems in a hurry.

[LADY CREECH and ALMERIC turn, startled. LADY CREECH haughtily sweeps away, entering the hotel.]

ALMERIC

[cheerfully]

Oh yes, possibly—he's off, you know—to catch a train. He's so easily worried by trifles.

[PIKE looks at ALMERIC with a sort of chuckling admiration.]

PIKE

Well, you don't worry—not too easy; do you, son?

ALMERIC

Oh, one finds nothing in particular this morning to bother one.

PIKE

[assenting]

Nothing at all.

ALMERIC

Not I. Of course, Miss Ethel is standing to her promise?

PIKE

[grimly]

Yes, she is.

ALMERIC

The Governor only thought it best to clear out a bit until we were certain that she manages to draw off this convict chap.

PIKE

[puzzled]

Draw him off?

ALMERIC

What you Americans call "affixing him," isn't it?

PIKE

"Affixing him?" Don't try to talk United States, my son. Just tell me in your own way.

ALMERIC

She's been giving him money, hasn't she? You took it to him yourself, didn't you? Naturally, we understood what it was for. She's trying to keep the beggar quiet.

PIKE

So that's what she sent this poor cuss the money for, was it?

ALMERIC

Why, what other reason could there be?

PIKE

Well, you know I sort of gathered it was because she was sorry for him—thought he'd been wronged; but, of course, I'm stupid.

149

ALMERIC

Well, ra-*ther*! I don't know that it was so necessary for her to hush him up, but it showed a very worthy intention in her, didn't it?

PIKE

[slowly]

Would you mind my being present when you thank her for it?

ALMERIC

Shouldn't in the least if I intended thanking her. It simply shows she considers herself already one of us. It's perfectly plain—why, it's plain as *you* are!

[Chuckles.]

PIKE

Oh! if I could only get it over to Kokomo! And that's why you're not worrying, is it, son?

ALMERIC

Worrying? My good man, do you mind excusing me. I saw a most likely pup yesterday; I'm afraid some other chap'll snatch him up before I do. I should have taken him at once. Good-morning!

[Exit through the grove with a sprightly gait and a wave of his stick.]

[PIKE gazes after him, shaking his head with a half-admiring, half-sardonic chuckle.]

[Enter ETHEL from the hotel. She wears a pretty morning dress and hat; her face is very sad.]

ETHEL

I hear that Lord Hawcastle has left the hotel.

PIKE

[dryly]

Yes; I saw him go.

ETHEL

He left very quickly?

PIKE

He did seem to be forgetting the scenery.

ETHEL

[decidedly]

He was afraid of Ivanoff.

PIKE

I shouldn't be surprised. Ivanoff wants to thank you. May I bring him?

ETHEL

Yes.

[PIKE goes off into the grove.]

[MARIANO and a file of servants enter from the hotel, form a line, and bow profoundly as VASILI enters. They withdraw at a sign from him.]

ETHEL

[making a deep curtsy]

Monseigneur!

VASILI

[to ETHEL]

Not *you*! You see, I must fly to some place where an incognito will be respected. If I stay here it will be—what you call—fuss and feathers and revolutionary agents. I have come to make my adieu to your guardian. Incognito or out of it, he is my very good friend—no matter if he is an egoist.

ETHEL

An egoist! That is the last thing in the world he should be called.

151

VASILI

Ah, so; what do you call him?

ETHEL

I? I call him—

[She begins bravely, but at a keen glance from him stops abruptly, blushing.]

VASILI

Bravo! I call him an egoist because he is so content to be what he is he will not pretend to be something else! I respect your country in him, my dear young lady; and he cares nothing whether I am a king or a commoner. Everywhere the people bow and salaam half on their knees to me; but *he*—

ETHEL

No, I can't quite imagine *him* doing that.

[Enter PIKE from the grove, followed by IVANOFF.]

VASILI

[to PIKE]

I have come to bid you goodbye, my friend. Life is a service of farewells, they say; but if you ever come to St. Petersburg when I am there you will be made welcome. Your ambassador will tell you where to find me.

PIKE

I know I'd be welcome; and if you ever get out as far as Indiana, don't miss Kokomo—the depot hackman will tell you where to find me, and the boys will help me show you a good time. You'd like it, Doc—

[He stops, horrified at his slip of the tongue.]

VASILI

I *know* that.

PIKE

I don't know how to call you by name, but I reckon you'll understand I do think an awful lot of you.

VASILI

[as they shake hands]

My friend, I have confided to you that you are a great man. But a great man is sure to be set upon a pedestal by some pretty lady.

[ETHEL turns away.]

It is a great responsibility to occupy a pedestal. On that account I depart in some anxiety for you.

PIKE

What do you mean?

VASILI

Ah, you do not understand? Then, my friend—what is it you have taught me to say?—ah, yes—then there is sand in your gear-box.

[VASILI gives his hand to IVANOFF quietly, bows deeply to ETHEL, and goes quickly into the hotel.]

IVANOFF

[turning to ETHEL]

Dear, kind young lady, your guardian has known how to make me accept the help you granted. He has known how because his heart is like yours, full of goodness. I shall go to London and teach the languages. There I shall be able to repay you—at least what you have given me in money.

ETHEL

Professor Ivanoff, are you following Lord Hawcastle and your wife?

IVANOFF

My wife exists no longer for me.

ETHEL

But Lord Hawcastle? Do you mean to follow him?

IVANOFF

[with great feeling]

No, no, no! I could not hurt his body—I could not. The suffering of a man is here—here! What is it *he* has of most value in this world? It is that name of his. Except for that, he is poor, and that I shall destroy. He shall not go in his clubs; he shall not go among his own class, and in the streets they will point at him. His story and mine shall be made—ah, but too well known! And that name of which he and all his family have been so proud, it shall be disgrace and dishonor to bear.

ETHEL

[sadly]

Already it is that.

IVANOFF

But I forget myself. I talk so ugly.

ETHEL

It is not in my heart to blame you. Your wrongs have given you the right.

IVANOFF

[kissing her hand]

God bless you always!

[He takes PIKE'S hand, tries to speak, but chokes up and cannot. He goes into the hotel.]

PIKE

There *are* some good people over here, aren't there?

154

ETHEL

When you're home again I hope you will remember *them.*

PIKE

I will.

ETHEL

And I hope you will forget everything I've ever said.

PIKE

Somehow it doesn't seem as if I very likely would.

ETHEL

[coming toward him]

Oh yes, you will! All those unkind things I've said to you—

PIKE

Oh, I'll forget *those* easy!

ETHEL

[going on eagerly, but almost tearfully]

And the other things, too, when you're once more among your kind, good home folks you like so well—and probably there's one among them that you'll be so glad to get back to you'll hardly know you've been away—an unworldly girl—

[she falters]

—one that doesn't need to be cured—oh! of all sorts of follies—a kind girl, one who's been always sweet to you.

[Turns away from him.]

I can see her—she wears a white muslin and waits by the gate for you at twilight

[turns to him again]

—isn't she like that?

PIKE

[shaking his head gravely]

No; not like that.

ETHEL

But there *is* some one there?—some one that you've cared for?

PIKE

[sadly]

Well, she's only been there in a way. I've had her picture on my desk for a good while. Sometimes when I go home in the evening she kind of seems to be there. I bought a homey old house up on Main Street, you know; it's the house you were born in. It's kind of lonesome sometimes, and then I get to thinking that she's there, sitting at an old piano, that used to be my mother's, and singing to me—

ETHEL

[smiling sorrowfully]

Singing "Sweet Genevieve"?

PIKE

Yes—that's my favorite. But then I come to and I find it ain't so, no voice comes to me, and I find there ain't anybody but me,

[swallows painfully]

and it's so foolish that even Jim Cooley can write me letters making fun of it!

ETHEL

You'll find her some day—you'll find some one to fulfil that vision— and I shall think of you in your old house among the beech-trees. I shall think of you often with her, listening to her voice in the twilight. And I shall be far away from that sensible, kindly life— keeping the promise that I have made,

[falters]

and living out—my destiny.

PIKE

[gravely]

What destiny?

ETHEL

I am bound to Almeric in his misfortune, I am bound to him *by* his misfortune.

[She goes on with a sorrowful eagerness.]

He has to bear a name that will be a by-word of disgrace, and it is my duty to help him bear it, to help him make it honorable again; to inspire him in the struggle that lies before him to rise above it by his own efforts, to make a career for himself; to make the world forget the disgrace of his father in his own triumphs—in the product of his own work—

PIKE

[aghast]

Work!

ETHEL

Oh, I am all American to-day. No matter how humbly he begins, it will be a beginning, and no matter what it costs me I must be by his side helping him, with all my energy and strength. Can you challenge that? Isn't it true?

PIKE

I can't deny it—that's what any good and brave woman ought to feel.

ETHEL

And since it has to be done, it must be done at once. I haven't seen Almeric since last night; I must see him now.

PIKE

[grimly]

He's not here just now.

157

[HORACE enters; stands in the doorway unobserved, listening.]

ETHEL

I've shirked facing him to-day. He has always been so light and gay, I have dreaded to see him bending under this blow, shamed and overcome. Now it is my duty to see him, to show him how he can hold up his head in spite of it!

PIKE

I agree, it's your duty—

ETHEL

[eagerly, but tremulously]

That means that you—as my guardian—think I am right?

PIKE

I agree to it, I said.

ETHEL

[excited]

Then that must mean that you consent—

PIKE

It does—I give my consent to your marriage.

ETHEL

[shocked and frightened]

You *do*?

PIKE

I place it in your hands.

HORACE

[vehemently interrupting]

I protest against this. She's talking like a romantic schoolgirl. And I for one won't bear it—and I won't allow it!

158

ETHEL

Too late—he's consented.

[With a half-choked, sudden sob she runs into the hotel.]

HORACE

[turning furiously on PIKE]

I tell you I shall not permit her to throw herself away!

PIKE

Look here, who's the guardian of this girl?

HORACE

A magnificent guardian you are! You came here to protect her from something you thought rotten; now we all know it's rotten, you hand her over!

[Turns with a short, bitter laugh, walks up stage, then comes back.]

By Jove! I shouldn't be surprised if you consent to the settlement, too!

PIKE

[solemnly]

My son, I shouldn't be surprised if I did.

HORACE

Is the world topsy-turvy? Have I gone crazy?

[With accusing finger pointed at PIKE.]

I'll bet my *soul* that'll disgust her as much as it does me!

PIKE

My son, I shouldn't be surprised if it would.

HORACE

[staring at him]

By the Lord, but you play a queer game, Mr. Pike!

PIKE

Oh, I'm jest crossing the Rubicon. Your father used to have a saying: "If you're going to cross the Rubicon, cross it. Don't wade out to the middle and *stand* there; you only get hell from both banks."

[Enter LADY CREECH from the hotel.]

LADY CREECH

[testily]

Mr. Granger-Simpson, have you seen my nephew?

HORACE

No; I've rather avoided that, if you don't mind my saying so.

LADY CREECH

Mr. Granger-Simpson!

HORACE

I'm sorry, Lady Creech, but I've had a most awful shaking-up, and I'm almost thinking of going back home with Mr. Pike. I rather think he's about right in his ideas. You know we abused him, not only for himself, but for his vulgar friend; yet his vulgar friend turned out to be a grand-duke—and look at what our friends turned out to be.

[Goes rapidly into the hotel.]

[ALMERIC'S voice is heard from the grove. "Come along! There's a good fellow!"]

LADY CREECH

Isn't that Almeric?

PIKE

Here he comes, shamed and bending under the blow!

[ALMERIC enters from the grove, leading a bull terrier pup.]

ALMERIC

Mariano, Mariano—I say, Mariano! I say, Aunty, ain't he rippin'? Lucky I got there just as I did—a bounder wanted to buy him five minutes later.

[MARIANO enters from hotel.]

Mariano, do you think you could be trusted to wash him?

MARIANO

Wash him!

ALMERIC

Tepid water, you know; and mind he doesn't take cold; and just a little milk afterward—nothing else but milk, you understand. You be deuced careful, I mean to say.

MARIANO

[with dignity]

I will give him to the porter.

[He carries the animal into the hotel.]

LADY CREECH

Almeric, really, there are more important things, you know.

ALMERIC

But you don't seem to realize I might have missed him altogether. I think I'm rather to be congratulated, you know. What?

PIKE

I think you are, my son. I have given my consent.

ALMERIC

Rippin'!

LADY CREECH

And the settlement?

161

PIKE

The settlement also—everything!

[ETHEL enters from the hotel, followed by HORACE.]

LADY CREECH

[greatly relieved and overjoyed, starting toward ETHEL]

Ethel, my dear!

ALMERIC

[cheerfully]

I told you it would all be plain sailing, Aunty. There was nothing to worry about.

LADY CREECH

[continuing, to ETHEL]

All shall be forgiven, my child. I am too pleased, too overjoyed in your good-fortune to remember any little bickerings between us. The sky has cleared wonderfully. Everything is settled.

ETHEL

Yes; it's all over; my guardian has consented.

ALMERIC

Of course *I* never worried about it—but I fancy it will be a weight off the Governor's mind. I'll see that a wire catches him at Naples—and he'll be glad to know what became of that arrangement about the convict fellow, too.

ETHEL

[very seriously]

Almeric, I think it's noble to be brave in trouble, but—

ALMERIC

[puzzled]

162

I say, you know, you've really *got* me!

ETHEL

I mean that I admire you for your pluck, for seeming unconcerned under disgrace, but—

ALMERIC

Disgrace? Why, who's disgraced—not even the Governor, as I see it. You got that chap called off, didn't you?

ETHEL

Whom do you mean?

ALMERIC

Why, that convict chap—didn't you send him away? You bought him off, didn't you, so that he won't talk? Gave him money not to bother us?

ETHEL

[rising, and turning on him indignantly]

Why, Heaven pity you! Do you think that?

ALMERIC

Oh—what?—he wouldn't agree to be still? Oh, I say, that'll be rather a pill for the Governor—he'll be a bit worried, you know.

ETHEL

Don't you see that it's time for you to worry a little for yourself? That you've got to begin at once to do something worthy that will obliterate this shame—to begin a career—to work—to work!

ALMERIC

[puzzled]

But? But I mean to say, though—but what *for?* What possible need will there be for an extreme like that? Don't you see, in the first place, there's the settlement—

ETHEL

[aghast]

Settlement! You talk of settlement, *now*.

LADY CREECH

[angrily]

Settlement, *certainly* there's the settlement!

ETHEL

What for?

LADY CREECH

Why, don't you understand—you're to be the Countess of Hawcastle, aren't you?

ALMERIC

Why—hasn't he told you?—the only obstacle on earth between us was this fellow's consent to the settlement, and he's just given it.

ETHEL

[dazed and angry]

Do you mean to say he's consented to that!

ALMERIC

Why, to be sure—he's just consented with his own lips—didn't you?

PIKE

[gravely]

I did.

LADY CREECH

Don't you see, don't you hear that—he's consented? He didn't mumble his words—don't you hear him?

ETHEL

I do, and disbelieve my own ears. Yesterday, when I wanted something I thought of value—and that was a name—he refused to let me buy it—to-day, when I know that that name is less than nothing, worse than nothing—he bids me give my fortune for it. What manner of man is this! And *you,*

[to LADY CREECH and ALMERIC]

what are you that after last night you come to me and ask a settlement?

LADY CREECH

[angrily]

Certainly we do—would you expect to enter a family like this and bring nothing?

ALMERIC

I can't see that the situation has changed since yesterday. I don't stick out for the precise amount the Governor said. If it ought to be less on account of that little affair last night—why, we should be the last people in the world to haggle over a few thousand pounds—

ETHEL

[with a cry of rage and relief]

Oh! That is the final word of my humiliation! I felt that you were in shame and dishonor, and, because of that, I was ready to keep my word—to stand by you, to help you make yourself into something like a man—to give my life to you. That you permitted the sacrifice was enough! Now you ask me to PAY for the privilege of making it, I am released! I am free! *I am not that man's property to give away!*

LADY CREECH

[violently]

You're beside yourself. Isn't this what we've been wanting all the time?

165

ALMERIC

But slow up a bit—didn't you say you'd stick?

ETHEL

Any promise I ever made to you is a thousand times cancelled. This is final!

[With concentrated rage, turning to PIKE.]

And as for you—never presume to speak to me again!

ALMERIC

[to LADY CREECH]

Most extraordinary girl—she's rather dreadful, *isn't* she?

LADY CREECH

[with agitation]

Give me your arm, Almeric.

[They go into the hotel.]

ETHEL

[to PIKE]

What have you to say to me?

[PIKE raises his hands slowly, with palms outward, and drops them.]

ETHEL

What explanation have you to make?

PIKE

None.

ETHEL

That's because you don't care what I think of you.

[Bitterly.]

Indeed, you've already shown that, when you were willing to give me up to those people, and to let me pay them for taking me! You let me romanticize to you about honor and duty and sympathy—about my efforts to make that creature a man—and you pretended to sympathize with me, and you knew all the time it was only the money they were after!

PIKE

[humbly]

Well, I shouldn't be surprised.

ETHEL

Didn't you have the faint little understanding of me enough to see that their asking for money, now—would horrify me? Didn't you know that your consenting to it, leaving me free to give it to them, would release me—make me free to deny everything to them?

PIKE

[slowly]

Well, I shouldn't be surprised if I *had* seen that.

ETHEL

[staggered]

You mean you've been saving me again from myself, from my silliness, from my romanticism, that you've given me another revelation of the falsity, the unreality of my attitude toward these people, and toward life.

PIKE

[placatingly]

No, no!

ETHEL

[vehemently]

You'd always say that, you'd always deny it—it's like you. You let me make a fool of myself and then you show it to me, and after that you deny it!

[Angrily.]

You're always exhibiting your superiority! Would you do that to the dream girl you told me of, to the girl at home who plays dream songs for you in the empty house among the beeches? Do you think *any* girl could love a man for that? Go back to your dream girl, your lady of the picture!

PIKE

[disconsolately]

She won't be there.

ETHEL

[stubbornly]

She *might* be.

PIKE

No, there ain't any chance of that. The house will still be empty.

ETHEL

[almost crying]

Are you *sure*?

PIKE

[sadly]

There ain't any doubt of it now.

ETHEL

You might be wrong—for once!

[She gives him a look between tears and laughter, then runs into the hotel.]

[PIKE stands sadly, his head bent, every line of his body expressing dejection; then from within the hotel come the sounds of a piano in the preliminary chords of "Sweet Genevieve." ETHEL'S voice is lifted in the song, at first faint, somewhat tremulous and quavering, then rising strongly and confidently. PIKE'S face, slowly upraised, becomes transfigured. He crosses the stage spellbound, to the hotel door with the look of a man in a dream. He falls back a step, looking in.]

* 9 7 8 1 6 4 7 9 9 8 9 4 3 *